7 pts

W9-BZI-719

Hispanic F

EDISON JR. HIGH LEARNING CTR

EDISON JR. HIGH LEARNING CTR

BLOOD *on the* RIVER

EDISON JR. HIGH LEARNING CTR.

Also by Elisa Carbone

Last Dance on Holladay Street

The Pack

Storm Warriors

Stealing Freedom

Sarah and the Naked Truth

Starting School with an Enemy

BLOOD *on the* RIVER

JAMES TOWN 1607

15195 97

ELISA CARBONE

EDISON JR. HIGH LEARNING CTR

VIKING

VIKING
Published by Penguin Group
Penguin Group (USA) Inc., 345 Hudson Street, New York, New York 10014, U.S.A.
Penguin Group (Canada), 90 Eglinton Avenue East, Suite 700, Toronto, Ontario,
Canada M4P 2Y3 (a division of Pearson Penguin Canada Inc.)
Penguin Books Ltd, 80 Strand, London WC2R 0RL, England
Penguin Ireland, 25 St Stephen's Green, Dublin 2, Ireland
(a division of Penguin Books Ltd)
Penguin Group (Australia), 250 Camberwell Road, Camberwell, Victoria 3124,
Australia (a division of Pearson Australia Group Pty Ltd)
Penguin Books India Pvt Ltd, 11 Community Centre, Panchsheel Park,
New Delhi - 110 017, India
Penguin Group (NZ), Cnr Airborne and Rosedale Roads, Albany, Auckland 1310,
New Zealand (a division of Pearson New Zealand Ltd)
Penguin Books (South Africa) (Pty) Ltd, 24 Sturdee Avenue, Rosebank,
Johannesburg 2196, South Africa

Penguin Books Ltd, Registered Offices: 80 Strand, London WC2R 0RL, England

First published in 2006 by Viking, a member of Penguin Group (USA) Inc.

3 5 7 9 10 8 6 4

Copyright © Elisa Carbone, 2006
All rights reserved

LIBRARY OF CONGRESS CATALOGING-IN-PUBLICATION DATA
Carbone, Elisa Lynn.
Blood on the river : James Town 1607 / by Elisa Carbone.
p. cm.
Summary: Traveling to the New World in 1606 as the page to Captain John Smith,
twelve-year-old orphan Samuel Collier settles in the new colony of James Town,
where he must quickly learn to distinguish between friend and foe.
ISBN 0-670-06060-7 (hardcover)
1. Jamestown (Va.)—History—Juvenile fiction. [1. Jamestown (Va.)—History—Fiction.
2. Virginia—History—Colonial period, ca. 1600-1775—Fiction. 3. Powhatan Indians—
Fiction. 4. Indians of North America —Virginia—Fiction.] I. Title.
PZ7.C1865Blo 2006
[Fic]—dc22
2005023646

Printed in the U.S.A.
Set in Janson
Book design by Kelley McIntyre

For those who were there

EDISON JR. HIGH LEARNING CTR

BLOOD *on the* RIVER

EDISON JR. HIGH LEARNING CTR

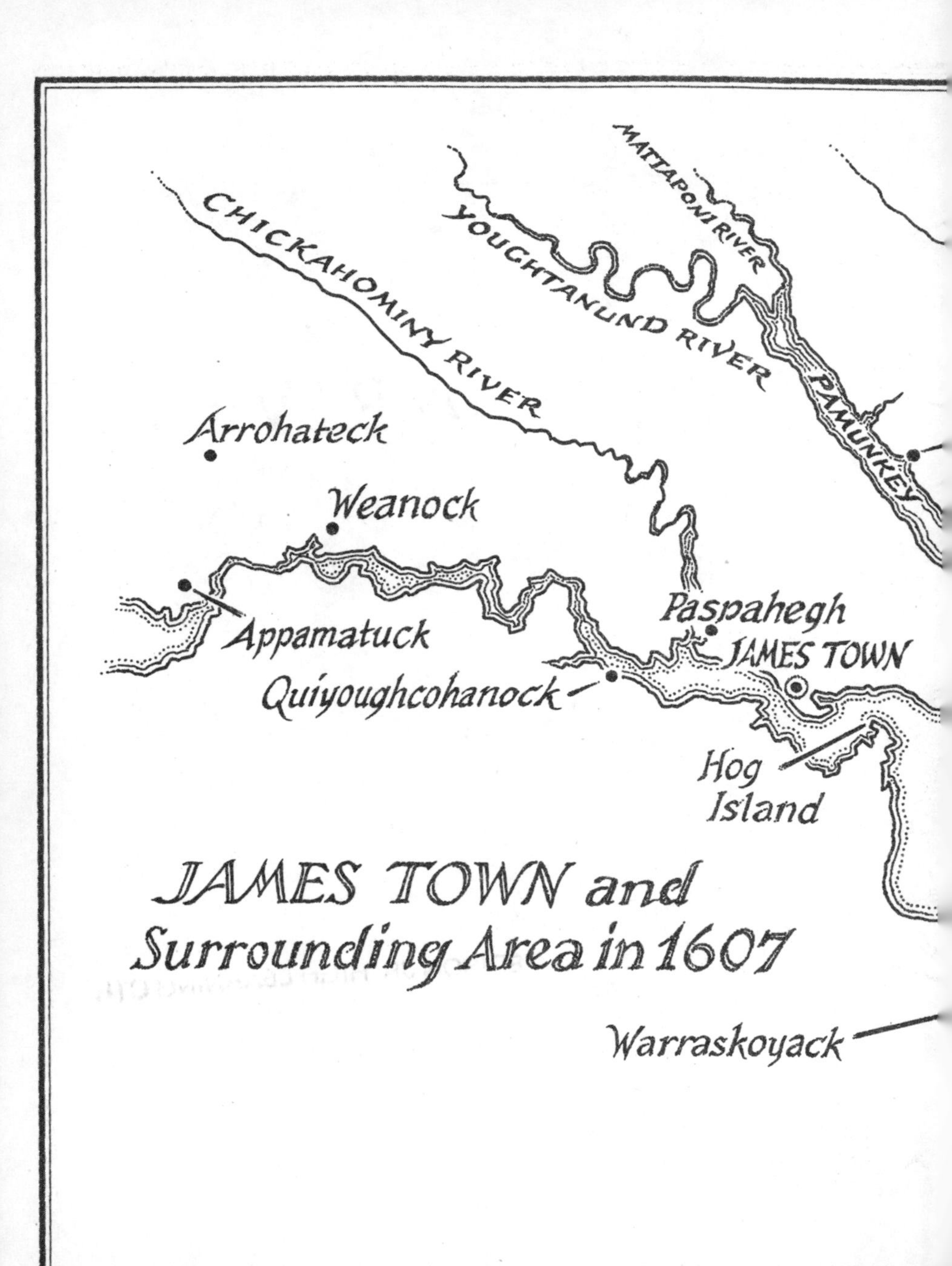
MATTAPONI RIVER
YOUGHTANUND RIVER
CHICKAHOMINY RIVER
PAMUNKEY
Arrohateck
Weanock
Appamatuck
Paspahegh
JAMES TOWN
Quiyoughcohanock
Hog Island
Warraskoyack
JAMES TOWN and Surrounding Area in 1607

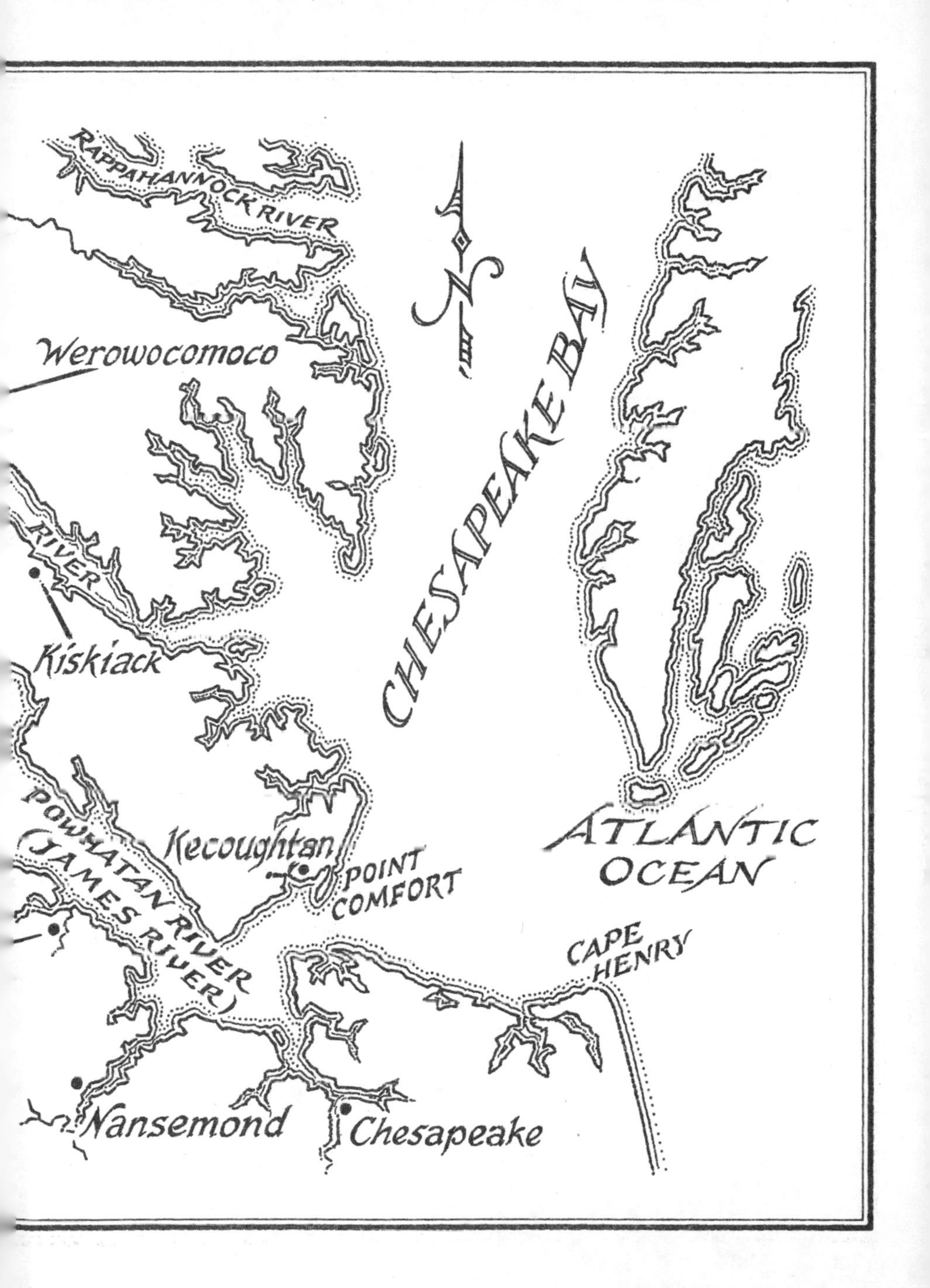

EDISON JR. HIGH LEARNING CTR

One

In the time of the first planting of corn
there will come a tribe from the bay of the Chesapeake.
This tribe will build their longhouses on the land of the Powhatan.
They will hunt and fish and plant on the land of the Powhatan.
Three times the Powhatan will rise up against this tribe.
The first battle will end and the Powhatan will be victorious.
But the tribe will grow strong again.
The Powhatan will rise up.
The second battle will end and the Powhatan will be victorious.
But the tribe will grow strong once more.
The third battle will be long and filled with bloodshed.
By the end of this battle, the Powhatan kingdom will be no more.

—Prophecy delivered to Chief Powhatan, ruler of the Powhatan empire, by his trusted priests, sometime before the Christian year 1607

London, England, October 1606

My feet slap, bare and cold, on the cobblestones. I'm breathing hard from running. I turn the corner—the street is dark, empty. It's my chance. I find the right door under the sign with three gold balls. I've carried a rock with me. I slam the rock down hard on the padlock, pounding until it breaks free. Inside the pawnshop it is quiet and musty. It smells of old wood and candle wax.

There is the locket, displayed on a piece of beaver felt. I close my fingers around the cool, smooth silver. I haven't touched it since the day she died.

Mine. It should have been mine, because it was hers. I pull, but it is wired down tightly.

I hear footsteps outside. I panic, yank on the wire—too hard. The wire slices my hand. I see my blood drip, but the locket is in my grasp.

"*You!* Boy!" A man lumbers into the shop—it's the shopkeeper come from his house across the street.

He lunges, grabs me, but I'm too fast. I squirm away and run, escape out into the fog, and I'm lost. Disappeared.

I walk along the docks, past the dark hulks of ships bobbing slowly. My heart is still racing. I try to calm myself. I listen to sailors laughing and arguing, their card games stretching into the night. I even venture a whistle—

nothing fancy, just my own tune. The shopkeeper will not find me, I promise myself. When he sees me in the daylight he will not know it was I who wrenched out of his grasp in the dark shop. And he certainly would never guess that I have not stolen anything, only taken back what is mine. It should have been given to me when she died, this locket of my mother's.

"This will bring a pretty penny," they said at the poorhouse. "It will pay for some of the extra food you eat."

Can I help it if I'm always hungry?

Then they expected me to stay on and keep working in the nailery, keep letting them beat me when they felt like it. As if I *wanted* to live in the poorhouse. As if Mum and I had wanted to be kicked out of our cottage on our farm. As if the blight was our fault and we wanted the crops to rot in the fields and had planned all along not to pay the rent to the lord of our cottage.

But I chose the streets instead. I'd rather dig in the garbage heaps with the rats for my meals.

Who knows? Maybe my mum would still be alive if she hadn't been a widow and hadn't had to work so hard—first for the greasy, fat gentleman who owned our farm and cottage, and then, after we'd been kicked off, making nails for twelve hours a day to pay our way at the poorhouse. Maybe she would still be alive if she'd had an easier time of it. Not my father, though. He would have drunk himself to death no matter what.

I find my favorite hollow near the London Bridge. Spiked on a pole atop the bridge is the severed head of a traitor—a man who betrayed the crown of England and paid for it with his life. I turn my face away so I don't have to look at those dull, staring eyes.

I curl up to go to sleep. For this one night, the locket is around my neck, hidden under my shirt. One night.

A SHARP KICK to the ribs wakes me.

"This looks like the one done it—scraggly hair and scrawny as a broomstick."

I'm on my feet in a split second.

"Grab him!"

I try to twist free, but hands close on my arms, my neck. It's the shopkeeper and his burly son.

I thrash and kick. They tighten their hold until it hurts. The shopkeeper pulls the locket out from under my shirt. "Ah, what have we here?" he says. A grin shows teeth brown as worms.

"It's mine," I cry. "*Mine!*"

They don't listen. They talk between themselves as they tie my arms behind me with ropes.

"The magistrate will enjoy this delivery—another criminal off the streets."

"The sooner he's hanged the better."

I throw my head back hard. It hits the son square in the chin.

"Yeow!" he cries. "He made me bite my tongue!"

He returns my blow. One swipe with his hand to the side of my head, just like my father used to do. And just like in the old days, I see black, feel my knees crumple, and I'm out before I hit the ground.

Two

On Saturday, the twentieth of December, in the year 1606, the fleet fell from London. . . .

—Master George Percy, *Observations Gathered out of a Discourse of the Plantation of the Southern Colony in Virginia*

SOME WOULD SAY I am lucky. Others would say I'm doomed. I escaped the gallows—that is why I am lucky. The magistrate mumbled something about having a son my age, pulled me out of my dark jail cell after just two days, and marched me down to the orphanage. "His name's Samuel Collier, age eleven, son of dead peasants. Can you take him?" he asked Reverend Hunt when he opened the orphanage door.

The reverend nodded to the magistrate and showed me to my bed in a row of neatly made beds.

Reverend Hunt is a tall, quiet man with broad shoulders and more patience than anyone I have ever known. He tells me I have a lot to learn about right and wrong.

"It was wrong to steal the locket," he says. "It was no longer yours—it belonged to the pawnshop owner." He says I need to make decisions based on love, not on anger.

"I loved my mum and wanted her locket back, so I *was* acting out of love," I say.

He just shakes his head. "The locket would not have brought your mother back," he says. I know he is right, and I know the real reason I stole it is that I was angry at the bosses at the poorhouse, angry at our landlord, angry at the world. But how can I make decisions based on love when there is no one left to love?

The orphanage was not a bad place—better than sleeping on the streets. Maybe if I'd been less of a danger to the other boys they'd have let me stay. But the boys started calling me "thief" and "jail rat" and I knew only one way to settle the argument: with my fists. Collin's nose spurting bright red blood was quite an accomplishment. But I think Richard's tooth only fell out because it was already loose when I punched him.

As for being doomed, if I am doomed then so is Richard. We are the two boys Reverend Hunt decided to bring with him on this journey to the New World. Richard is to be the reverend's servant, and I am to serve a man called Captain John Smith.

It is early on a December morning as we walk from the orphanage to the docks. Fog hangs thick and cold. It makes the stone houses drip and the wattle and daub houses look soggy. Richard carries Reverend Hunt's satchel, heavy with his books and Bible and some extra clothes. My new shoes clomp on the cobblestones. The shoes are too big—passed on from an older boy who died at the orphanage last month—but Reverend Hunt says I can't go barefoot in the New World.

The New World. The boys—Collin and the others—think we will die there. They even begged Reverend Hunt not to go. The reverend explained to them the importance of the mission. King James has granted a charter to the Virginia Company of London to send men to the New World, to Virginia. The men will explore for gold, silver, and jewels, and for a new passage to the Orient, and they'll cut down New World trees to send back to England to build English houses—all to make a big profit for the investors of the Virginia Company. But the real importance, Reverend Hunt says, is to bring the good news of Christ to the native people who live in Virginia. He says we'll also look for survivors from the Roanoke colony, the settlers who went to Virginia with Sir Walter Raleigh over twenty years ago. That is why Reverend Hunt wants to go. But I want to go for the gold. They say it washes up on shore with every tide.

We reach the harbor. The sky is gray with morning light, and the place is alive with commotion. Hawkers call out their wares, and I smell fresh baked bread. Sailors pull on ropes and pulleys, lifting barrels to swing from each ship's yard arm so they can be loaded onboard. Officers shout orders, and sailors march up the gangways carrying loads on their shoulders. Reverend Hunt points out the three ships that will be ours. Their hulls and scaffolding are newly painted in rich blue, deep maroon, and pale yellow. He says the largest one is the *Susan Constant*, next in size is the *Godspeed*, and the smallest, a pinnace, is the *Discovery*. They bob next to the docks, and I watch as crates of chickens are carried on board.

I scan the throng of men milling around the docks. There are hoards of gentlemen dressed in velvet and silk, sailors in their wide-legged slops, and one very dirty boy selling eels. I wonder where he is, this Captain John Smith. Reverend Hunt says he is a soldier, an officer—not a ship's captain but a captain in the English military. And he is a commoner, a yeoman, so I don't look for him among the gentlemen.

I am to be Captain Smith's page, which means I'm supposed to serve him *and* learn from him. I don't argue with Reverend Hunt, but inside I scoff at the idea. Me, an apprentice to an officer? I've never been teachable in my life. Except my mum teaching me how to read—that, I sat still for. But my father tried to teach me smithing, and when I ruined a piece of iron, out came his fist. I won't have some man I hardly know trying to beat sense into me.

A man comes marching up, his face flushed red with anger. A sword hangs by his side, and his cape flies as he walks. "They're sending nothing but gentlemen!" he shouts at Reverend Hunt. "By God, who will build the houses? Who will grow the crops? Do they think they can *eat* the gold and silver they are hoping to find?" He spits on the ground. "I know these gentlemen. They'll expect to have everything done for them, expect it to be easy. They won't lift a finger to work."

Reverend Hunt speaks calmly, lays a hand on the man's shoulder. "John, there are carpenters going, too, and laborers, and these boys, and—"

"*More* gentlemen than commoners!" the man shouts. "The investors of the Virginia Company were raving *mad* when they chose the men for this journey." Then, suddenly he seems to notice me and Richard. "Is this the boy you promised me? Which one is the fighter?"

Reverend Hunt nods my way. The man, who I think must be Captain John Smith, narrows his eyes at me. I narrow my eyes back at him. I have a moment to study him while he studies me. Not tall, but stocky and strong. Curly reddish-brown hair and beard. Flashing green eyes. *If you beat me I'll spit in your ale*, I threaten silently.

Captain Smith smiles slightly, almost as if he has heard my unspoken threat. "Yes," he says slowly. "We'll take that energy you've got for fighting and put it to some good use." He turns to Reverend Hunt. "At least we'll have a good worker here."

Is that what he plans for me? To make me into a work-horse? I cross my arms over my chest and scowl.

Captain Smith looks about at the crowd. "Where is Captain Newport?" he asks impatiently. "I want to speak to him about this gentleman problem." He marches off, leaving us behind.

Reverend Hunt turns to me and Richard. "There are men here whom you must show extra respect to, you understand?"

Richard and I both nod. I have never seen so many finely dressed gentlemen in one place.

"Over there." Reverend Hunt points discreetly with his chin. "Sir Edward Maria Wingfield. A very high-ranking gentleman, and a member of the Virginia Company. Remember who he is."

I take a good look at Edward Maria Wingfield. He's got a puffed-out chest and a strut like a peacock. *Wing*field, I say to myself, imagining him with bright tail feathers and wings. I won't forget.

"And there," Reverend Hunt says. "Captain Bartholomew Gosnold, captain of the *Godspeed*."

I already have birds on my mind, so I think of a *gos*ling

with light-colored down to match Captain *Gos*nold's fair hair.

"And him," Reverend Hunt says. "That's Captain John Ratcliffe, captain of the *Discovery*, the smallest ship."

Captain Ratcliffe has close-set, beady eyes and a long, pointy nose. "*Rat*cliffe," I whisper, and have to bite my lip to keep from snickering.

"And over there is Captain Christopher Newport. He's captain of the *Susan Constant* and leader of the whole expedition. Do not forget who he is."

I see Captain Smith talking to a tall, dark-haired man in a red doublet. The man's right sleeve is pinned up and empty. I remember the boys at the orphanage talking about Captain Newport, how he was in a battle at sea with the Spanish and got his arm shot off. I would think that the loss of an arm would diminish a man, but I see that it has not diminished Captain Newport one bit. He nods to Captain Smith, then looks over the scene around him with an air of confidence and authority, as if it were his kingdom. In fact, these three ships and all of the men on board *are* his kingdom until he drops us colonists safely in the New World.

"Now wait here," Reverend Hunt tells us. "I'm going to find out which ship we'll be on."

Richard and I stand there but we don't talk. Richard is younger than I am by a year, and a bit shorter and broader, with dark, serious eyes. We haven't said a word to each other since I knocked his tooth out. This suits me just fine; I don't need a friend. I haven't needed anyone since my mum died.

Reverend Hunt returns and tells us we'll be passengers on the flagship, the *Susan Constant*. A breeze picks up. It will be a good day for sailing.

"Get your men on board," Captain Newport orders.

I feel a leap of excitement inside me. Doomed or not, the adventure is about to begin.

Three

The fifth of January [1607], we anchored in the Downs. But the winds continued contrary so long that we were forced to stay there some time, where we suffered great storms.

–Master George Percy, *Observations*

I RUB MY EYES and blink in the dim light of the 'tween deck. The ship pitches and rolls. I only know it's morning because of the bit of light that peeks in around the gun ports and the closed hatch, and because the roosters and hens down in the hold know, and they have started a racket.

The 'tween deck reminds me of the root cellar at the orphanage, with its close walls and ceiling. It is one long room running almost the length of the ship, though one can hardly walk for the barrels and crates that are taking up most of the room. At first, a few of the gentlemen hung pieces of cloth to make partitions, since they thought they deserved some privacy, but those have all come down now in favor of setting up crates as card tables and barrels as sitting stools for their card games.

The chickens are luckier than we are—most days their crates are brought up on deck and they get fresh air to breathe. And the ship's cats and two dogs have the run of the place. So do the ship's one thousand rats. We passengers are only allowed up to empty slop buckets or get the stew pots for our meals. Captain Newport says he doesn't want us getting in the sailors' way up on deck.

We are all seasick. And bored. And we are going absolutely no place. We have had nothing but storms and winds blowing the wrong direction for weeks now, and so we sit anchored in the cold, close enough to see England's shores but still trapped down in this hole of a 'tween deck with the stench of urine and vomit and chicken dung. The gentlemen complain constantly. They want to sail back to shore and go home. Sir Edward Maria Wingfield is the most vocal in his complaints. He is furious at Captain Smith, who keeps reminding the gentlemen that they have signed seven-year contracts with the Virginia Company, and they can't quit this voyage. I can see why Master Wingfield wants to quit—even living on the streets was better than this.

Next to me, sleeping in our bed—a straw-and-canvas

mattress thrown over some barrels—are Richard and snot-nosed, nine-year-old James. James is servant to the gentleman George Percy, and afraid of everything. The men sleep two to a bed, but all three of us boys are crowded in together. There is a fourth boy, Nathaniel. He is older than I am, probably thirteen or fourteen. It's a good thing he's on one of the other ships, or they'd have us sleeping four to a bed.

I kick James to wake him. "Give me some room, you little worm."

James groans and rolls over. He leaves a smudge of snot on the canvas. "I am not a worm," he whines sleepily.

Everyone is waking up now. I hear yawning, grunting, men relieving themselves into slop buckets.

"James, bring me my wash water. *Now.*" Master Percy is not a patient man, and James has to hop up to fetch water even before he has a chance to rub the sleep out of his eyes.

Richard is still sleeping. He is the soundest sleeper I have ever seen. Not even roosters crowing and men clomping right by his ear wake him. But Reverend Hunt is very ill with the seasickness and he will need help. I jostle Richard hard. He groans but doesn't open his eyes. *Fine,* I think, *let him get a lecture on slothfulness from Reverend Hunt.*

James and Richard have become good friends to each other even though James is a gentleman's son and Richard is a commoner. They are not my friends, though. I have kept my distance, from them and from everyone else on board the *Susan Constant*. Instead of trying to decipher which of the men are to be trusted and which are not, I have made it simple for myself: *Trust no one*. It is a philosophy that worked for me in the poorhouse, on the streets of London, and at the orphanage. I see no reason to change.

Captain Smith has not beat me yet. He does not seem inclined to, but you never can tell. There is not much required of me aboard ship, just to bring him his wash water in the morning and empty the slop buckets we all use. There is not much for any of us to do. That is why there is so much time for the bubbling up of discontent. And today is the day it boils over.

"I have had enough," Master Wingfield announces. "The food is monotonous and salty, the commoners stink, and the storms will not cease. We will sail back to London at once. Who is with me?"

"Aye!" several of the gentlemen call out.

"We are with you. We're ready to turn back."

Captain Smith stands and addresses them. "Are you all *cowards*?" he demands. "And are you *liars*? Were you lying when you signed your contracts with the Virginia Company?"

I cringe. Captain Smith is especially angry today, and I know he has gone too far. I have seen how these gentlemen wield their power when they are insulted.

Master Wingfield answers Captain Smith in a low growl. "You have forgotten your place, Mr. Smith."

"They should never have sent you gentlemen on this voyage!" Captain Smith nearly shouts it. "You're all weak, every one of you. You know nothing about survival."

Master Wingfield is livid. I think he is about to thrash Captain Smith. I would like to see a fight, but Reverend Hunt steps in. Sick as he is, Reverend Hunt calms Master Wingfield down and talks about how God wants us to bring Christianity to the New World. He somehow makes a fragile peace, somehow convinces the gentlemen to wait just a little longer for an east wind. But I know there is no peace inside Master Wingfield. I know it is only a matter of time before he strikes. It will not be with his fists, as we commoners do. It will be with his power, and it will be worse than fists.

Four

Travel south until your butter melts, then turn right.

—Old British mariner's axiom:
How to get to the New World

February 1607

My soul nearly left my body last night. I felt it, slippery and shimmery inside the shell of my body, trying to slide out through the top of my head. But Reverend Hunt came and laid his hands on my brow to keep my soul from leaving, and prayed for me to recover. And so today, my fever has broken and I am still in my body, still aboard the *Susan Constant*, bound for the New World.

We are finally sailing. I feel the speed of the ship

under me. We have left England's waters, and we're heading south toward the Canary Islands off the coast of Africa. Captain Newport says our route will be like a big circle, following the winds and currents. We'll sail south to the Canaries, then west to the West Indies, and then north to Virginia. To go back to England—if I ever do—we will sail still farther north and then east to England to finish the circle.

Captain Newport says the fevers gripped us because we stayed so long in the fog and cold of England's winter. Now it is warmer every day.

If my soul had gone out of my body, I'd have left the rolling of the ship, the stench in the closed-up 'tween deck, the rats that sometimes scuttle over my face in the night. I'd have left this living shoulder to shoulder with a crowd of gentlemen, each of them thinking he's better than the rest, and *all* of them thinking they are much better than I. But I'd also have left the chance to see the islands and, beyond them, Virginia. I'd have left my chance to dig for gold. So if it hadn't been for Reverend Hunt and his big, meaty, soul-blocking hands, last night I would have joined my mother in heaven, or my father in hell, and missed the whole exciting adventure of it.

I pull on my slops and tie them at my knees and at my waist. I'm so skinny now, they nearly fall off of me. How long was I ill? Ten days? Two weeks? I wobble on unsteady legs. Air. That's what I need, fresh air. Someone throws open the hatch. This is my chance. I pick up a slop bucket—my ticket to the ship's deck.

I start up the ladder carrying the slop bucket carefully. I glance down into it: human waste and vomit sloshing together. Bad idea. I feel woozy, almost lose my balance. *Look up*, I tell myself, and I do, and in a moment my head is out of the hatch opening and I'm looking at a violet-blue sky with wispy pink clouds. Sunrise at sea.

"Look at what the cat dragged in," a sailor calls. He's pulling on a thick line and looking down at me from the foredeck. "Haven't seen this one in weeks. Thought maybe he'd died."

"Stinks bad enough down there," says another sailor. "Could be a few dead ones lying behind the ale barrels and no one would even know!"

The sailors laugh, but I don't care. I stand, breathing in the clear, fresh air. I go to the railing, throw the contents of the bucket overboard, and then stop in utter astonishment. I stare, unbelieving. The ocean, which just a few weeks ago in England was its usual black-green, has completely changed. I am looking at an ocean so clear and so blue that when a long silver fish comes to inspect what I have just tossed in, I can see the yellow stripes on his back. I linger, feeling the wind on my face. The sails are bellied out orange-gold in the early morning sunlight. I feel very glad that I did not leave this adventure last night.

"Below with you, now," a sailor yells to me. "You'll be getting underfoot up here."

I want to tell him I'm waiting for the mess pot for the servants, the one that James and Richard and I share with the two men who serve Master Wingfield. But I'm not sure I can make it down the ladder with the heavy pot of oatmeal. I'll wait until I'm stronger before I do that chore.

Captain Newport comes strutting toward me. He has a scowl on his face, and I'm afraid he's about to whip me for loitering on deck. I scramble down the ladder, bucket in hand.

Captain Newport follows me. He swings down the ladder easily, even with only one arm. I head to a dark corner of the 'tween deck, hoping he won't see me.

But it's not me he's after.

"Smith." Captain Newport's baritone voice fills the 'tween deck. Two burly sailors come down the ladder and stand on either side of him.

"Sir," Captain Smith responds, and stands straight and strong.

Captain Newport looks angry, though I'm not sure it's Captain Smith he's angry with. "By my authority as captain of this fleet, I hereby place you under arrest."

Captain Smith frowns. "On what charges?" he demands. He stares right at Master Wingfield as he says it, so I suspect he knows who has accused him of a crime.

Captain Newport glances at Master Wingfield with a look of disgust.

"I will present the charges," says Master Wingfield. Somehow, despite the fact that we've been at sea for nearly two months, his silk doublet and velvet breeches still look relatively fresh. "You are under arrest for intent to overthrow the government of this mission, murder the council members, and make yourself ruler."

My mouth drops open.

"Wingfield, you are a *liar,*" Captain Smith growls.

"And you, sir, will be hanged when we reach the West Indies," Master Wingfield says coldly.

Captain Smith sputters, but no words come to him. His face and neck are red as fire. He reels back. I see his fist ball up. He's about to throw a punch.

Yes! I want to shout. *Smash his face in!* This will be even better than watching boys or drunken sailors slug it out. I want to see blood spurt out of Master Wingfield's high-ranking nose.

But in the split second before Captain Smith lets loose with his fist, it is as if something reins him in. He hunches his shoulders, opens and closes his hands, takes a deep breath. Then he turns to Captain Newport and speaks almost calmly.

"Captain, do you believe these charges which have been brought against me?" he asks.

Captain Newport looks startled, as if he didn't expect

this question. "I . . . I cannot leave a suspected traitor unshackled," he says.

"And what if I accuse Master Wingfield of being a traitor?" Captain Smith asks. "After all, it was he who wanted to turn back when we were stranded all those weeks at the Downs. It is he and his *gentleman* friends who want to go back to England, to their comforts, every time there is a storm." He says the word *gentleman* as if it is a pile of sheep dung in the kitchen, and this makes me smile. "This is how they treat their *signed* seven-year contracts with the Virginia Company."

"You have no right to accuse me!" Master Wingfield shouts. "You are a commoner! You cannot level charges against your betters."

"My betters?" Captain Smith raises his eyebrows. "A pig has more royal blood than you do."

The sound Master Wingfield makes next is a cross between a growl and a shout. Insulting his bloodline is like throwing lye in his face. He draws his dagger and comes at Captain Smith.

For a moment, all is confusion. Reverend Hunt catches Master Wingfield's arm, the two sailors step between the angry men, and Captain Newport's voice booms out. "Release your weapon. Let the law handle this." Then he orders the sailors, "Nellson, Poole, put Smith in irons!"

The two sailors hustle Captain Smith over to the chain bolts that stand ready, fastened to the wall of the 'tween deck, waiting to restrain a prisoner or any drunken sailor who has started a fistfight. They clamp Captain Smith's ankles and wrists into the chains.

I can't believe Captain Newport is doing this—now Master Wingfield will simply walk over and slit his throat! But when I look back at Master Wingfield, I see he is pale and shaken. He has dropped his dagger and is wiping his face with his handkerchief. Reverend Hunt has his hand on his shoulder and is talking to him quietly. Master Wingfield might be a liar, but he is no murderer.

Still, I have heard the gentlemen whispering. In the close quarters of the 'tween deck, it is hard to miss much. They say Captain Smith is only an ignorant commoner, and yet he wants the power of a noble. They say he will try to take over the whole mission if he is not disposed of. They say if it were not for Captain Smith insisting that they stay the course, they would be back in their comfortable homes in England by now. And I wonder how long it will be before someone else, someone who does have the heart of a murderer, slits Captain Smith's throat while he sleeps.

Five

We anchored at Dominico . . . a very fair island . . . inhabited by many savage Indians. . . . They are continually in wars, and will eat their enemies when they kill them, or any stranger if they take them.

–Master George Percy, *Observations*

EVERY SOUND WAKES ME. I crane my neck—is *this* the night someone will murder Captain Smith? But each time it is only one of the men groaning in his sleep, or the retching of one of the poor souls who has not yet gotten over the seasickness. And so, Captain Smith is still alive.

We anchor at one of the Canary Islands—Gran Canaria. I steal a chance to go on deck and have my first sight of land in many weeks. Huge gray mountains, steep and rocky, rise up into the clouds. A few of the sailors go ashore in the longboats to fill our barrels with fresh water, and then we are on our way, riding the trade winds west toward the West Indies in the Caribbean.

Captain Smith is still in chains, though they have freed his wrists and only his ankles remain shackled. When I bring him his morning wash water, he is writing. I glance at the page, then quickly look away. I don't want to be caught being nosy.

He washes his face, takes off his shirt, and washes under his arms. I hand him a cloth to dry with. When he is dressed again, he looks at me hard.

"Reverend Hunt says you can read?" he says. It is a cross between a question and a statement.

I nod my answer.

"He tells me your mother taught you. But your mother was a commoner, a peasant, correct?"

"Yes, sir."

"Can you tell me how it is that she learned to read?" he asks.

"She was taught by a friend, sir. It was the son of our gentleman landlord." I don't tell him that he also gave her the silver locket when she turned thirteen or how, when their friendship was discovered, he was sent away to France.

"I see," he says, and goes back to his writing.

I wonder how Captain Smith can be so peaceful while he is locked up like this. Since the moment when he nearly punched Master Wingfield, the moment when he reined in his anger, Captain Smith has been calm. That first day he had me bring him his paper, quill, and ink. "When Julius Caesar was put in prison, he *wrote*," he said. "So I shall do the same." He has been writing ever since—the story of our journey. As he writes and remains calm, the whisperings have changed. Now they say that Master Wingfield and some of the other gentlemen made up those charges. They say those gentlemen hate Captain Smith because he is a commoner who has no special respect for nobles. They say you can't hang a man just because he doesn't respect you. In a strange way, even though he is still a prisoner, Captain Smith seems to be winning the battle.

James and Richard come down the ladder, talking the whole way. Richard is carrying the oatmeal pot for our mess, and James has a slop bucket he has just emptied. Captain Smith doesn't need me anymore, so I hurry toward the steaming pot of oatmeal. I have to eat fast to get enough. We servants are always served last, when the food is running out, and Master Wingfield's servants, Henry and Abram, are big, greedy men who empty our mess pot in two gulps if we boys don't get a head start. I grab my spoon and dig in.

"Yes, that's what he said," Richard is saying. "They don't wear any clothes at all. They just paint themselves different colors instead. The sailor said he heard it from a French sailor who has already been to the New World."

"What else?" James asks.

"That the women make cuts and burns on their faces and bodies to make pictures on them. Then they put colored dyes in the cuts and burns. They think it makes them look beautiful."

I snicker and nearly spit out my oatmeal.

Richard gives me an annoyed glance. "He said that the men have hair a yard long on one side of their head and the hair is shaved close on the other," he says. "And they decorate their hair. One of their favorite decorations is they cut off the hand of one of their enemies and dry it in the sun and then tie the dried hand into their hair."

Henry and Abram join us. Henry is broad and fleshy and always enjoys an opportunity to smack one of us boys. Abram has hair the color of carrots and one eye that wanders everywhere except where he is looking. When they sit down to eat, James and Richard are silent for a while as they shovel oatmeal into their mouths. There is a plate with five chunks of moldy cheese on it. I go to grab the largest chunk, but Henry slaps my hand away and takes it for himself. I want to slap him back, but he is three times my size and could easily throw me against the wall with one swipe of his arm. I grab a smaller piece of cheese and stuff it into my mouth, green mold and all.

"They also said there will be Carib Indians on the islands in the West Indies," Richard continues. "They said the Caribs chop people up for their cook pots and eat them."

Now James looks pale and terrified.

Henry snorts. "Don't worry, lad. They don't want you. You're too skinny and snotty for their taste." He slaps James on the back hard enough to hurt, then he and Abram go off to their card game with the other common men.

"What else did you hear?" I mock Richard in a singsong voice. I can hardly believe he is so gullible that the sailors are able to fool him like this.

"It's true, you know." Richard glares at me. "I heard the sailors talking. I heard it all with my own ears."

James nods, his eyes wide and scared.

"You are dunces, both of you, believing that rot," I say. "Don't you think the sailors knew you were listening? Don't you think they're up there right now laughing their heads off about that stupid boy who was eavesdropping and believed all their lies?"

Richard and James exchange a look.

"You think they were lying, Samuel?" James asks me hopefully.

"I think you're an idiot," I say. "Those sailors are playing games with you. They're almost as bored up there as we are down here." I look at Richard. "Do you really think a woman would make cuts and burns in her face to look beautiful?"

Richard frowns, then shakes his head.

"Then stop talking about it," I say.

Moments later we hear the call, "Land ho!"

Richard grabs the empty oatmeal pot, but I yank it out of his hands.

"Hey, that's *my* job," he shouts. "I brought it down."

"It's my job now," I say. I run to the ladder with the pot. No way I'm going to let this chance slip by.

Up on deck I squint in the dazzling sun. The sails billow bright white against a blue sky. The breeze is warm. I go to the railing and search the horizon. There it is: a green bump in the distance, in the midst of the jewel-blue sea. The first of the Caribbean islands. I give the pot to the cook and linger, breathing in the sweet air, marveling at the brightness of it all. Richard comes up on deck, and James, too, and several of the gentlemen, until the first mate calls a halt. He drives us all back down below, threatening to beat us boys with an oar if we don't hurry.

The 'tween deck is abuzz with gentlemen and commoners both, wondering what this land sighting means.

"Will we finally be allowed off this stinking ship?"

"They'd better at least get fresh water. What we have left smells like a sick dog."

"I want fresh meat. I will demand that I be let off to hunt."

When the shouting begins up on deck, we all fall silent.

"God, save us, they're coming!"

"Look at them. They're monsters!"

"Captain Newport, permission to man the guns, sir."

James and Richard both look at me as if I have the answers. I decide I'd rather be beaten with an oar than sit in the dark 'tween deck waiting to be devoured by sea monsters. I scramble up the ladder to the deck.

We are in shallow water now, and the sea is a translucent blue. Moving swiftly across this crystal water are several canoes. In the canoes are the very creatures conjured up by Richard's stories. They are naked, their skin painted red. The women's faces and arms are tattooed with patterns, the men's hair is long with beads and bones—human bones?—hanging in decoration. They are coming quickly toward our ships.

I catch my breath. I expect to hear the scrape of the cannons being loaded, but instead I hear Captain Newport's voice: "We are *not* Spanish barbarians. We will not slaughter these people . . . unless they attack first. Get Smith. *Now!*"

Two sailors swing down into the 'tween deck, and there is the clanking of chains as they unlock Captain Smith's irons. Captain Smith emerges from the 'tween deck. He stands on the deck watching the approaching canoes. His back is straight, his chest puffed out. He does not look afraid, only determined.

A tall man stands up in one of the canoes. He is naked

except for a ring of bones around his neck. He raises his hand. Captain Smith does the same.

Captain Smith begins speaking strange words and using hand motions to communicate. I easily understand the hand motions. We come in peace (hand over his heart). We desire trade (he dangles several strings of sparkling beads). We need food (he rubs his stomach).

The man in the canoe stoops and picks up something that looks like a very large pinecone with spiky green shoots coming out of one end. He pretends to take a bite out of it. I breathe a sigh of relief. He has understood.

All afternoon, the natives come back and forth to our ships in their canoes, bringing sweet-smelling fruits and other food from their island, which sits, green and lush, nearby. The large pinecone with spiky leaves turns out to be called a "pineapple," and it tastes like food for a king. The cook names the other things they bring: mangoes, papayas, plantains, potatoes, tobacco. In return we give them knives and hatchets, beads, and copper, and they are happy.

I have seen that Captain Smith's ankles are raw from the rubbing of the irons. That evening I ask the cook for some tallow and bring it to him.

"Are you a free man, sir?" I ask.

"I seem to be for now," he says. He grimaces as he rubs in the tallow. The sores on his ankles are cracked and oozing.

Quietly, I ask, "How did you know the language of those natives?"

He smiles. "Every man speaks the language of greeting, of trade, of hunger. I spoke with my hands."

I nod. "But the words . . ."

He shakes his head and whispers, "Those are Algonquian words—a language spoken in Virginia by the natives there. Roanoke settlers brought back word lists, and I have studied them. Let Newport and the others think they need me as a translator in these islands. It's too hot for those chains."

I have one more question, but I am not sure if I want to know the answer. I take a deep breath and blurt it out. "Do the Carib Indians chop people up for their cook pots and eat them?"

He stops rubbing his ankle for a moment and looks at me. "Only if they catch them," he says.

Six

Whilest we remained at this island we saw a whale chased by a thresher and a swordfish; they fought for the space of two hours. We might see the thresher with his flail lay on the monstrous blows, which was strange to behold. In the end these two fishes brought the whale to her end.

—Master George Percy, *Observations*

THESE ISLANDS ARE strung together much like beads on a necklace. When we sail past one, in half a day we catch sight of another. I sneak up on deck so often my back is sore from being smacked with that oar. But the sky and water are so blue and everything is so new, I keep coming up anyway.

It is hot. We boys and common men abandoned our shoes, stockings, doublets and slops weeks ago. Now even the gentlemen go around with their white, knobby knees peeking out from under their long shirttails.

We anchor near the island of Guadeloupe, and Captain Newport takes several men ashore to explore. While the boats are anchored, we passengers are allowed up on deck, and so I stand at the railing to watch the longboats glide through water clear as turquoise glass. A strong hand closes on my arm and I startle. It is Captain Smith.

"*Look*," he says, pointing.

A huge black form comes racing through the sea. Close behind it are two smaller forms.

"It's a type of whale—the biggest fish in the sea," Captain Smith says. Then he smiles strangely. "It is being chased."

The three fish disappear behind the *Discovery*, then reappear on the other side.

"What would chase a *whale*?" I ask.

"Looks like a swordfish and a thresher shark," says Captain Smith. "We will see who wins."

The whale surfaces and spurts out a spray of air and water. In that moment, the thresher rears up its tail and lands a tremendous blow on the whale's snout. The whale is stunned. He tries to escape, but the swordfish swims in to cut him. Bright red blood swirls into the clear water. The thresher lands another harsh blow, and another. The whale becomes confused, swims in circles. The swordfish darts in and out, cutting and slicing. Soon the once-blue water is murky with blood. As the whale slows, the thresher deals more slamming blows and the swordfish cuts again and again. Finally the whale rises to the surface, spurts a stream of spray one more time, then rolls over, belly skyward.

Captain Smith has a satisfied look on his face, as if his regiment has just won a battle. "You see how it is when you've left the confines of England?" he asks me. "You might have been *born* the biggest fish in the sea, but the skill and perseverance of those lower born can take you down and *destroy* you."

Somehow I know that he is talking about Master Wingfield, the biggest fish in the sea. I glance around to see who else has heard. I see Master Clovell glaring at us, and I wonder how long Captain Smith will remain unshackled if he keeps talking this way about the gentlemen.

"LAND HO!" I hear the familiar shout. It must be another island. But then I hear more.

"Is this where we'll drop anchor, Captain, and take all the men on shore?"

"Yes. Have the bosun ready the longboat."

I run up on deck. They'll be too busy now to catch me. The day is a rare overcast one, and the sails reflect the gray of the sky. The *Susan Constant* turns, sailors rush to pull on lines, and we are on our way, gliding in to shore. As we get closer I see the tall trees. They've got huge green leaves at their tops, and their bare trunks curve upwards like fingers reaching for the sky. I see a bright green-and-yellow bird fly from one treetop to another.

Land. I wonder if I'll remember how to walk on it.

"Fetch the tents!"

"Lower the longboat."

"Men, gather your belongings. We are going ashore."

I gladly—very gladly—help load bedding, tents, pots, and pans onto the longboat to be taken ashore. The *Godspeed* and the *Discovery* anchor nearby as well, and their men unload. This will be the first time since we left England that all of us—all 105 of us men and boys who are passengers, and three crews of sailors—will be together in one place. There are probably Carib Indians on the island, Captain Newport tells us, but we will give them beads and our soldiers will stand guard at night, and we'll be safe.

I'm one of the last to go ashore. When I finally stand on the white sand, it feels as if it is moving under me. I laugh out loud. More than three months on a ship has confused my legs so much that solid land feels like the rocking deck!

"Samuel, look. We're Carib Indians!" James calls to me.

He and Richard have taken off their shirts and they're running naked through the water, splashing each other. I have been waiting for James or Richard, or both, to tell me how I was wrong and they were right about the Caribs. But neither of them has. I have been on my guard, ready to rough them up if they say one word about it. Are they taunting me now, showing me what naked Caribs look like, telling me I was wrong not to believe them?

"Come on, Samuel." James stands in waist-deep water, dripping wet. His skin is peaked pale, and his fair hair is plastered against his head. "It's salty," he says, and licks some water from his hand. "It's fun. Come swim with us."

I blink at him. No taunting? No insisting they were right and I was wrong? No hating me for how badly I have treated him and Richard this whole journey? I wonder if James can really be this forgiving, or if he is simply so happy to be off that stinking ship that he has forgotten the past.

"Come on in, you prig," calls Richard. "You need a good delousing."

That makes me mad. "You're the one who brought the lice onto the ship!" I shout. I yank off my shirt and charge into the water. I splash Richard in the face until he begs for breath. When I stop, he is gasping. He smiles a little, as if he wants to pretend it was fun, but I know it was not. My eyes dare him to try and splash me back. Or insult me again. I know he will not. He doesn't want to lose another tooth.

"Stop, you two," James whines. "Look at the fish!" He tries his best to distract Richard and me from our quarrel.

I feel tickling on my legs. When I look down into

the clear water, I see small blue-and-yellow fish nibbling on me. The water is warm—so much warmer than the Thames.

"I want to live here forever," says James. "I'd never go back to my stepmum ever. She would think I'd died, and that would make her happy."

"I want to stay here, too," says Richard. "I wouldn't be cold ever again."

I shake my head. "I still want to go to Virginia," I say. "There's a sack of gold waiting for me there. Maybe ten sacks."

Reverend Hunt calls to us from shore. "Boys, come here. Put your shirts on. The sun will burn your skin."

I wish we didn't have to leave the water, but we do what Reverend Hunt says. Disobeying him would be like disobeying God.

When we get to shore, he is holding our shirts and three wide-brimmed straw hats. "The sun here is like ten English suns," he says. "You put these on."

Reverend Hunt waits while we pull our shirts over our heads and tie the hat strings under our chins. "Now," he says. "There is work to be done. There are the tents to be set up, the cook wants all the pots scrubbed with sand, and Captain Ratcliffe wants a path cut to the baths. They've found hot baths in the forest, and he says the gentlemen can't be tromping through the underbrush to get to them."

Captain Ratcliffe of the beady eyes and pointed nose. Captain Smith grumbles that he doesn't see why the gentlemen can't walk through the forest like anyone else, but Captain Ratcliffe has the power to give orders, not Captain Smith.

When we join the others I see the older boy, Nathaniel. He is holding a hatchet. He must be on his way to help clear the path.

I don't want to scrub pots like a woman, so I hurry to get one of the hatchets, too. I swing it a few times to feel its weight and power. I want to do a man's job.

Henry, Abram, Nathaniel, and several of the sailors start toward the forest with their hatchets. I follow them.

"What do we have here?" Henry turns to look at me, then stops to block my way. "A scrawny chicken coming to work with the men?"

I don't answer. I want to say I wouldn't be so scrawny if he'd leave more of the food for me. I try to skirt around him and continue on my way, but he puts out one powerful arm to stop me. "Go back and scrub pots with the other boys," he growls. "You'll only get in the way." He yanks the hatchet out of my hands and cuffs me.

I glare at him silently as he turns and walks after the others. What is he going to do with two hatchets? I hope he chops himself in the leg.

Reluctantly, I go find the cook. He is already hovering over Richard and James, showing them how to scoop up a handful of sand with a rag and use it to scrub out the mess pots. They haven't had a really good cleaning in three months, so the sand has some hard work to do. I join them, toiling under the hot sun until sweat drips from my face. I wish I could be back playing in the salty sea, or swinging a hatchet in the shade of the forest.

Suddenly a scream comes from the forest—a man's scream of pain. Soon there is another cry, and then such shouting and shrieking, it turns my blood cold. I remember Captain Smith's answer when I asked if the Caribs chop people up for their cook pot. *Only if they catch them.*

"The path cutters!" I shout. "It's coming from that direction."

Gentlemen and soldiers grab their weapons and hurry toward the terrible sound. James and Richard huddle together behind the largest cook pot. I spot a sword and belt someone has left lying in the sand. Quickly, I try to fasten the belt around me. It's too big. I pull the sword out of its sheath and with the bare sword I run toward the sound of the battle.

Down the newly cut path I go, high-stepping over stumps and roots, following the soldiers and gentlemen. We all converge on the path cutters. They are yelling and writhing as if they are fighting invisible demons. Henry is hopping, swatting his arms and neck, shouting in agony. There is not a Carib Indian in sight.

"What is this?" Reverend Hunt demands, his voice booming over the cries. "What is happening here?"

"Fire!" Henry cries. "It feels like fire!"

I jerk my head around, searching the jungle. Have the Caribs attacked and run off? Or is it some strange beast? I hold out my sword, ready to fight. But I see nothing.

The hatchets are all on the ground. Reverend Hunt reaches to pick one up.

"No, Reverend, don't touch it!" It's Captain Smith's voice.

Angry red welts are rising on Henry's arms and neck, on Abram and the others, too. "To the baths!" Captain Smith orders them. "That will give you some relief."

They take off running, swatting at themselves as they go.

"It's the manchineel tree," Captain Smith says when things have quieted down. "The Caribs use its sap to poison their arrows and it burns like fire. Our men must have chopped into it."

I am impressed with Captain Smith's knowledge. As a soldier, he has already traveled the world, and has learned so much.

Tromping up the newly cut path at that moment is Captain Ratcliffe. His face is dripping with sweat.

"This all happened," Captain Smith says loudly, "thanks to Captain Ratcliffe and his ridiculous idea of a gentlemen's path."

Captain Ratcliffe wipes his brow and scowls. It looks to me as if he would spit in Captain Smith's face if he weren't so overheated. The two men stare at each other, fuming.

"Let's go, everyone, back to your work," Reverend Hunt says. With a wave of his hands he gets the men moving. It somehow breaks the standoff between Captain Smith and Captain Ratcliffe.

Captain Ratcliffe calls after the men, "I want a new crew to cut the path. Just leave those blasted manchi-whatever trees alone."

Captain Smith shakes his head and mumbles angrily under his breath.

I walk back toward the stack of mess pots waiting to be scrubbed. I carry the sword I borrowed. Captain Smith comes up behind me.

"That needs cleaning," he says.

It startles me. I give him a sideways look. Then I understand he means the sword. The metal is tarnished and even rusting in some places.

"I will show you how to clean it, and when you return it, the owner will thank you," he says.

On the beach Captain Smith demonstrates to me how to clean the sword with a rag and sand—he says this sand is fine enough to do the job. It is surprisingly similar to cleaning and polishing mess pots.

He orders me to do as he has shown me. I reach for

the rag. Then I stop. What if I do it wrong? Will he beat me, make a fool of me? I lower my hand. It is better to remain unteachable.

"If you will not obey me," Captain Smith says in a low, cold voice, "there are other, crueler men you may serve instead."

I clench my teeth. Nothing to do but try. I reach slowly for the rag again, scoop up sand, press it against the sword blade and give it a stroke. I forget to be care ful—my finger slides along the blade. I yelp, stick my sliced finger into my mouth, suck on the blood.

Captain Smith laughs. "Ah, I cut my fingers many times learning to clean a sword. Let me see it," he says.

I hold out my finger. It is still bleeding, but the cut is not so deep that it will stop me from using my hand.

Captain Smith rips a strip off the rag and ties it tightly around my finger. "Try again," he orders.

I look up at him. I did it wrong, and yet he did not beat me. I pick up the rag again. I am careful of my fingers this time. I give a short stroke, and another, and another. Soon the rust and the tarnished spots have turned to shine. They gleam in the late afternoon sun.

Captain Smith nods. "Good," he says. "Now return it to its owner before one of these lazy gentlemen calls you a thief."

I run off to find the belt and sheath. They are still lying in the sand. I return the sword to its place.

That evening I hear hammering, and after a while I go to see what is being built. Have some of the gentlemen decided they need *houses* instead of tents to sleep in?

When I see what it is, my mouth goes dry: a wooden frame, a rope hanging from the highest beam, a noose tied in the rope. Master Wingfield has not forgotten his promise to hang Captain Smith.

Seven

Such factions here we had as commonly attend such voyages, that a pair of gallows was made, but Captain Smith, for whom they were intended, could not be persuaded to use them.

—Captain John Smith, *The True Travels, Adventures, and Observations of Captaine John Smith*

THE NEXT MORNING dawns clear and warm. Captain Smith is back in chains, and the gallows sits ready.

Reverend Hunt calls us together for Sunday services. We meet, gathered around the tree where Captain Smith is chained so that he can join us. Reverend Hunt's sermon goes on for hours. I think maybe he will not stop until every single one of us has promised never to sin again. He says to tell a lie is a sin, and that any man who lies for his own gain and does not repent will spend eternity in the agony of hell's flames. He looks right at Master Wingfield and Captain Ratcliffe, delivering his sermon with passion. I see Master Wingfield squirm. Captain Ratcliffe sets his jaw and stares straight ahead. Captain Newport looks at the two of them and shakes his head. I send up a prayer that Reverend Hunt's sermon will save Captain Smith from his hanging.

After services I bring Captain Smith some food. I wonder if it will be his last meal. Yet, he is calm.

"I've been a prisoner before. And I escaped before," he says. "When I was a soldier, fighting the Turks of the Ottoman Empire, I was captured and made a slave. They shaved my head, put an iron ring around my neck, and brought me to auction to be sold like a beast."

James and Richard are nearby, and they come closer to listen.

"The other slaves told me it was useless to try to escape. Impossible, they said. But one day we were working in the fields. I was threshing wheat with a threshing bat. My master rode up on horseback with his whip. He cracked the whip, brought it down on my naked back, lashed my skin open. I was enraged. I took my threshing bat in both hands and swung." He swings his arms as if knocking the cruel master from his horse once again. "Down he came, and before he could get his footing, I cracked the bat over his head. Then I beat him with the stub until there was no life left in him."

No wonder Captain Smith is unafraid of these pale,

weak gentlemen and their threats. If he wants to, he will kill them with his bare hands.

"Then I shucked off my slave rags, put on my master's clothes, and rode off on *his* horse to *my* freedom," Captain Smith finishes his story.

The three of us boys are silent. I admire his courage. And I admire the way he talks back to the gentlemen as if they have no right to lord it over him. I've never known another commoner who had the nerve to do that.

Reverend Hunt comes marching up, a ring of keys dangling. He takes the keys to the clamps on Captain Smith's ankles. "I've convinced them that without you as translator, we will all perish in Virginia," he says as the clamps open and fall away.

"Thank you, Reverend," Captain Smith says, rubbing his ankles. "I owe you a favor."

Reverend Hunt gives him a stern look. "This is the favor I want, then. I want you to at least *act* as though you have the proper respect for these gentlemen. If you insult them and anger them again, they may choose their pride over their survival in the New World."

Captain Smith nods, and I wonder if he really does plan to be polite to the exalted gentlemen from here on in. He is at least as stubborn as I am, so I know it will be hard for him to change.

That afternoon the sound of chopping wood rings out over the rumbling of the waves. The gallows is cut up and thrown on the fire, where it nicely roasts our fish for supper.

AFTER SIX DAYS on Nevis I am fatter. The birds are so tame we pluck them out of the bushes with our hands, the sea is teeming with fish, and the trees are full of fruit. The only natives on the island are afraid of us and they stay well hidden. I am also cleaner. I have gone twice to the hot pools in the forest to bathe.

But now Captain Newport says it is time to leave. We pack up the tents and cook pots, barrels we have filled with fresh water, meat and fish we have dried for the rest of our voyage, and crates full of pineapples, mangoes, plantains, coconuts, and wild bird eggs.

We sail past the Spanish islands of Vieques and Puerto Rico. We stop on the island of Mona just long enough to get fresh water and for a group of gentlemen to go hunting. They leave in the morning, taking a few soldiers with them for protection from the natives. They dress as if they are going pheasant hunting on a cool English morning, in silk doublets, velvet breeches, stockings, shoes, and felt hats, with their powder flasks hanging at their sides. The group returns in the evening, exhausted and faint, carrying what the expedition has killed: two boars, several iguanas, and the gentleman Edward Brookes. They say Brookes's fat melted inside his body in the extreme heat.

Captain Smith has a few choice words to say about gentlemen who are too ignorant to know they should carry enough water on a six-mile hike in the tropics, and too ignorant to take off their extra clothing when they get hot. But this time he is wise enough not to utter these words where any of the gentlemen can hear him.

I did not know Edward Brookes well. He was a passenger on one of the other ships. Still, it is strange to see his pale, waxy skin, and his limbs stiff with death.

They dig a shallow grave for Master Brookes, and we sail away, leaving him there on Mona. I have dreams that night that the cannibals find his body, dig him up, and eat him. I awake in a cold sweat. I try to calm down, reminding myself that this could not possibly happen. No one digs up a grave for food.

Eight

The six and twentieth day of April, about four o'clock in the morning, we descried the land of Virginia.

–Master George Percy, *Observations*

THE 'TWEEN DECK seems dark after all those sunlit days on the island. We are sailing north now, toward Virginia. Reverend Hunt says we will travel right past Florida without stopping because it belongs to the Spanish. He says that forty years ago the French had a colony at Fort Caroline in Florida. He tells me how he heard that the Spanish came and massacred all of the French settlers—men, women, and children. No, we will not be foolish enough to land at Florida.

Foul weather makes the 'tween deck even darker. Thunder cracks, loud as a cannon shot. I look up through the hatch opening and see black storm clouds boiling in the sky.

"Take in the sails!" Captain Newport orders.

Another crack of thunder booms and lightning flashes. I hear the wind whip the rigging against the masts. The sea bucks, and the ship rolls and jerks. Men begin to retch again as if they were new to seafaring. The rain comes down in torrents, and when we shout that it is flooding the 'tween deck, the sailors oblige us by covering up the hatch so that we are shut in the dark with only stale, vomit-scented air to breathe.

Lanterns are lit, and they swing wildly, making shadows move like ghostly dancers. The gentlemen complain bitterly. We should go back to England, they say. We should have reached Virginia weeks ago. We must be off course. This voyage is ill-fated.

I lie in my bed, angry and discouraged. Captain Newport has been telling us for weeks that we'll see land any day. Maybe we *are* off course. I am sick of the 'tween deck, sick of sailing, sick of the storms that come one after another. And this is the most violent storm yet. The sound of crashing waves is a roar in my ears, punctuated by the creaking of the wooden ship.

James and Richard lie next to me. "Are we going to die?" James asks. "Will the waves break open the hull?"

I hear a loud crack and it makes me jump. It is followed by frantic squawking, and I realize it is only a chicken crate that has smashed into an ale barrel down below. "Shut up, James," I snap at him. I am annoyed that he could scare me into mistaking a sliding chicken crate for a cracking ship's hull. "Yes, you are going to die. Every one of us is going to die," I say.

James begins to whimper, and I am sure he's dripping snot onto the bed.

"Aw, do you want your stepmum now?" I taunt him.

Richard sits up and slugs me in the arm. "Stop it," he shouts over another rumble of thunder. "Leave him be, you—you stinking jail rat. You're nothing but a common thief!"

In a second I'm up on my knees. I'm pounding Richard with my fists, punching his face, his shoulders, anywhere I can hit. He is kicking, flailing. He kicks me in the stomach, and I can't breathe. James scoots out of our way and wails for Reverend Hunt. In the shifting shadows, it's hard to see. I swing. My fist connects with Richard's teeth, and I feel my knuckles cut open. Now Richard is on his feet; he whacks me in the side of the head. I feel dizzy, but I jump up, ready to meet him toe to toe.

Strong arms close around my chest, dragging me back, away. I see Richard's face, blood dripping from his mouth, down his chin.

It is not Reverend Hunt who has dragged me away. I will not get a sermon on how fighting is not the Lord's way, how I must learn to act from love instead of anger.

No, it is Captain Smith who has hold of me. I know better than to struggle. He drags me to where the chain bolts lie, then releases me.

"Stand on one foot," he orders.

I hesitate a moment, thinking this is a stupid thing he has ordered me to do. He cuffs me for my hesitation. It is the first time he has hit me, and it makes me want to run. But there is no place to run to.

"Stand on one foot!" he shouts.

I can do this ridiculous thing or be cuffed again, harder. It is difficult to balance on the rocking ship, but I try. I lift my left leg, balance on my right. The ship lurches; I stumble, catch myself. I try again, fall against a barrel.

"Do it!" Captain Smith orders. He is glowering at me. "Stand on one foot, you fool!"

Tears catch in my throat. He is worse than my father. I lift one leg. I balance for a split second, but Captain Smith shoves me and I fall onto the 'tween deck floor. I shout in frustration.

He stands over me. "Does it work, Samuel?" he demands. "Can you stand on one foot when a storm rocks the ship? Can you keep your footing when I shove you?"

I am bewildered and angry. I shake my head. No, I cannot balance on one leg in a storm.

Captain Smith picks up the chains that recently held him prisoner. "In London it might have worked for you, this standing on your own, treating other boys as if they don't matter. In Virginia, it *will not work*, do you understand me? The wilderness is like a ship in a storm. We will need one another to survive." He clamps the irons roughly around my ankles and wrists. "If these blasted gentlemen refuse to learn that fact, then at least my page *will* learn it. This colony will need to stand on many legs if we are not to be toppled over in the Virginia wilderness."

He goes back to his own bed, and I am left to try to find a comfortable way to sleep in my chains, between two crates.

"LAND HO!"

The shout comes before dawn. It is followed by a loud ruckus up on deck: whooping and hollering, laughing and stomping. Everyone on the 'tween deck is awake in an instant.

Captain Smith calls across to Reverend Hunt. "Reverend, did you pray up that storm last night? From the sounds of it, it blew us straight to Virginia!"

I am cold and stiff from sleeping chained, curled up in a small space like a snail. I rub my eyes. My head hurts and my jaw aches. I need a slop bucket badly, and there is none within reach. I'm too proud to call for help, though, so I grit my teeth and wait.

Someone lights a lantern and men begin to stir. Reverend Hunt marches Richard over to me. His cheek is swollen, and one of his eyes is turning purple. I am proud of my handiwork.

Richard looks at me, and I see a half-smile cross his face. I realize I must be purple and swollen, too, for him to look so satisfied.

Reverend Hunt clears his throat. "Richard has something to say," he tells me.

Richard twists his shirttail around his fingers. "I'm sorry I hit you," he says quickly. "And I won't call you those bad names anymore."

I wonder if he means it, or if he is just obeying Reverend Hunt. But mostly I am hoping someone will figure out that I need a slop bucket before I soil my slops.

Captain Smith ambles over. "As I remember, it was important for someone to bring me a bucket in the morning when I was locked in those things," he says, and yawns. "But Samuel doesn't need anyone's help, so I suppose we'll just leave him be. That's the way he likes it."

The three of them start to walk away. I am about to burst. I jump to my feet. "Captain Smith, sir!" I call after him. "Might I please have a slop bucket?"

Captain Smith looks at me and laughs. "Me, an officer, serving my own page? I think not."

I dance from one foot to another. Why is he tormenting me? I certainly can't ask Reverend Hunt to bring it to me. Then I understand. Richard is the only one I can ask, the only one who should be asked to bring a slop bucket to another servant. I groan. I can't wait much longer or I'll be embarrassed beyond words, *and* have no clean slops to wear. "Richard!" I try to keep the desperation out of my voice. "I am sorry for punching you last night. Bring me a bucket, would you?"

Richard glances at Captain Smith and grins, enjoying his moment of victory. But Captain Smith puts a quick stop to the gloating. "Don't make the boy wait—hop to it," he says.

The moment Richard sets the bucket down, I drop my slops, have a seat, and relieve myself.

Captain Smith seems satisfied with what I have learned about cooperation, and he unclamps my chains. "Don't let your anger get the best of you, Samuel," he says. "Learn to channel it, and it will become your strength rather than your weakness." I have seen that he has been channeling his anger at Master Wingfield and Captain Ratcliffe into his writing. He is telling *his* side of the story.

I turn my attention to the excitement at hand—have we really found Virginia? Master Wingfield pounds on the closed hatch. "I demand to know what is happening up there!" he shouts.

Finally, the sailors pull open the hatch and send down reports: We have entered a bay; there are tall trees along a sandy shoreline. There is no sign of savages. Then they tell us we're dropping anchor. A party will go ashore to explore.

At last we are allowed up on deck for our first sight of Virginia. It is green, quiet, and desolate. There are no natives coming to us in canoes as they did in the Caribbean islands. There are no houses, no huts, just wise old trees in spring leaf, standing guard over the sandy shore. Quiet, desolate, and *free*. We can pick any place, any piece of forest or meadow, and make it ours.

A group of gentlemen and sailors get ready to go ashore.

"Bring picks and shovels," Master Wingfield orders.

Captain Smith scoffs. "I suggest we find a place to *live* before you go digging for gold. We can't eat gold."

Master Wingfield gives him a disdainful look. "Did you not read your contract with the Virginia Company? The part where it says we are to turn a profit for the company as soon as possible? We will eat the supplies we brought, and dig for gold."

The *Godspeed* and the *Discovery* are anchored nearby as well. I watch as the longboats are rowed to shore. About thirty men in all disembark for the exploratory trip, most of them gentlemen and sailors. Many of them have their muskets ready with slow matches burning.

Those of us who are left spend the day sitting or lying around either on deck or in the 'tween deck, waiting. And while we wait, the gentlemen, soldiers, carpenters, laborers, and servants all discuss their ideas about the New World.

"You can't get gold in a day. We'll need to plow and plant and live here awhile."

"You won't catch me walking behind a plow. I've got peasants to do that back in England. I say we eat the stores we've brought, get the gold fast, and go home."

"The gold is not where the biggest profit is. I want to explore—find the new passage to the Orient the Virginia Company wants. Now that's how to strike it rich. If we can get goods—silk, spices, and jewels—from India and China back to England without having to deal with those Ottoman Turks and their marked-up prices, just think of the profits we will make!"

And there is one lone voice, Reverend Hunt, who says he has not come for gold or to find the new passage to the Orient. He says we have been sent by God for more noble purposes: to bring the good news of Christ to the Virginia natives, and to look for survivors from the Roanoke colony. Of course, as soon as he says it, all the other men agree that that's some of why they have come as well. But I know their hearts are set more on gold and profits than on finding lost colonists or saving souls.

James and Richard have gotten hold of a deck of cards and are playing and laughing. I am determined to stay out of trouble, so I don't say one mean thing to them all day. When I look at the quiet forest I wonder what it will be like to live there, to build houses and create a settlement. I wonder what it will be like to do as Captain Smith says and work *with* the others rather than keeping to myself the way I have done for so long. It seems to me it will be strange, and I'm not sure I will like it.

The cook starts supper. He throws a large chunk of pork and several pounds of peas with water into the cook pot. Later, he adds handfuls of sea biscuits. They are hard enough to break your teeth when they are dry, but in the pease porridge they will become soft and chewy.

At dusk we hear voices and look out to see the men returning. They are in good spirits, and I wonder if they've found gold already.

"Just in time for supper," declares the cook, and he begins to ladle pease porridge into the mess pots.

Suddenly I hear a cry, then frantic shouting and someone moaning. I run to the railing. In the half-light of dusk I see them, five of them, crouched on a hill, their naked bodies painted, arrows flying from their longbows. Already one of the sailors has fallen.

"No!" I shout, as if my voice, my objection, can change anything. "Use your muskets—*shoot* them!"

I hear the command, "Make ready your piece!" Our men load their muskets: prime the pan, charge the piece with powder, put in the musket ball, ram down the charge, cock the match. . . .

But by the time the first musket shot rings out, the

Indians are already leaving, creeping away silently on hands and feet like bears. The musket balls don't even come close to them.

The injured men are brought to Dr. Thomas Wotton, aboard the *Godspeed*. A gentleman, Gabriel Archer, has been shot through both hands, and a sailor has been shot twice in the torso.

I see now that this land is not so free and open. This is Indian land, and they do not want us here. And what is worse, it seems to me that their bows and arrows are quicker, more accurate, and can shoot farther than our muskets.

Nine

Now falleth every man to work: The council contrive the fort; the rest cut down trees to make place to pitch their tents, some provide clapboard to relade the ships, some make gardens, some nets, etc.

—William Symonds, ed., *The Proceedings of the English Colony in Virginia*

HAVE WE CROSSED the wide ocean only to be shot by the natives the minute we set foot in Virginia? We servants gather around our mess pot, but no one eats much. James is crying, sniffling, with snot running into his mouth. "I want to go home," he whimpers.

Richard keeps his eyes cast down. "Reverend Hunt said we'd tell them about the Bible," he says softly. "He didn't say they'd want to kill us."

Henry slaps him on the back with a loud thwack. "You can't believe everything you hear, my boy."

Abram's wild eye is vibrating off to the side. I try not to look at him.

After supper I go to find Captain Smith. He is sitting with his quill and paper, writing. Now he can add that we finally landed in Virginia, but that the natives do not want us here. I stand, waiting quietly. He finishes filling a page, blots the ink carefully, then looks up at me.

"Yes, Samuel?"

"Sir, how will we make a settlement if this is Indian land? Will we have a war?"

He pats a barrel next to him and bids me to sit down. "The men who came back to England from the Roanoke colony wrote about the Virginia Indians. They are interested in trade, and we have brought the things they prize: copper, metal tools, glass beads, needles, mirrors, and such. It will be a delicate balance, but if we can find a piece of land they are not using, and come to them in peace with goods to trade, I believe we can settle here without a war." He scratches his beard, thinking. "We must do it without a war. There are many more of them than there are of us."

That night as we bed down, I feel the rocking of the ship. I try to imagine that we are still out at sea rather than anchored near this strange new land of Virginia. I wonder if Collin and the other boys at the orphanage were right, that Richard and Reverend Hunt and I will all die here.

THERE IS A BOX we carried with us that was not to be opened until we reached Virginia. It contains the names of the men chosen by the Virginia Company to be our leaders, and directions for us from the Virginia Company. Captain Newport gathers the other ship captains and high-ranking gentlemen on the *Susan Constant* and opens the box. As he reads the names, at first there are no surprises: The men on our council will be Edward Maria Wingfield, John Ratcliffe, Christopher Newport, Bartholomew Gosnold, John Martin, and George Kendall. But when he reads the last name on the list it causes a big ruckus. That name is John Smith.

"He is still under arrest," Master Wingfield objects. "The fact that he is out of his chains does *not* mean his name has been cleared."

"He's a criminal!" Captain Ratcliffe declares.

They raise such a fuss that Captain Smith is not allowed to become a council member.

I think Captain Smith would make a better leader than most of the men on the council, but what I think does not matter. Captain Smith seems determined to stay out of trouble, just as I am, and he accepts the council's decision without a fight. To me, in private, he says, "You will see how quickly they will be begging me for help and advice."

Captain Newport reads more of the orders from the

Virginia Company: Be careful in choosing a site for the settlement—go up the river where you can keep a lookout, so the Spanish cannot mount a surprise attack; take great care not to offend the Virginia natives, and begin trading with them for food right away; do not write letters home that say anything bad about the New World—people in England must not hear a single thing that would discourage them from coming to Virginia.

A few carpenters and sailors go onshore and put together the shallop, a small boat meant for exploring that we brought with us in pieces. Then a group of gentlemen go off to search for a place for us to settle. The reports they come back with are encouraging: They have met lots of natives and have been welcomed into their villages, invited to eat with them and watch their dances. They say we do not need to fear the natives. When I look at Captain Archer's bandaged hands I hope they are right.

They are also mapping the land and water. They say they have found a point of land with deep water all around and named it Point Comfort. They have planted a tall cross at the mouth of the bay where we first landed and named the place Cape Henry. The only discouraging news is that they have seen no sign of survivors from the Roanoke colony.

Then, finally, on May 13, 1607, seventeen days after we first landed in Virginia, our explorers bring us the news we have been waiting for: They have chosen a place for us to settle. It's a place where the river is deep close to shore so it will be easy to moor our ships to trees. It's got fresh water from the river, rabbits, squirrels, birds, mussels, oysters, fish, crabs, strawberries, and mulberries. It's safe from the natives because there are none living nearby. We'll also be safe from the Spanish because it's on a peninsula and we'll be able to see any approaching Spanish ships for miles down the river. They've named the river the James, in honor of King James of England, and our settlement will be called James Town. The council votes and selects Master Wingfield as our first president.

We sail upstream and moor the ships near our chosen site. They seem small, bobbing in the river beneath towering old trees. Their paint of blue, maroon, and yellow, so rich when we began this journey, is now faded and chipped. They have weathered nearly five months at sea, and they show it.

As the sun sets, I gaze at what will be our new home. There are high bluffs just upstream, but our site has a sandy shoreline along the river. The trees wave their branches in the breeze, and a huge gray bird circles, calling out his objection to our presence. We bed down for one last night on the *Susan Constant*.

I lie awake most of the night, excited, a bit scared, wondering, waiting for the first rooster crow to signal time to go ashore. The morning of May 14, even Richard is up and ready before sunrise.

I dress quickly and go up on deck to help load the longboat. We pile in as many men and goods as we can, and then the sailors take to the oars and row to shore. When it is my turn, I ride with several of the common men and most of the chicken crates. We unload the crates and set the chickens free to peck around this New World.

I wander off a bit before anyone can give me my next task to do. I go a little way into the forest to look around. The trees are so tall I feel as if I am in a cathedral. I breathe in the rich smell of damp earth. The leaves are a bright early spring green, and sprinkled along the ground are tiny flowers of white, yellow, and violet. Butterflies and dragonflies add to the riot of color. *I am either in a cathedral or in paradise*, I think.

Captain Smith finds me and hands me a straw hat and a hatchet and tells me to get to work. We will begin felling the smaller trees in order to make room for our tents and gardens. James and Richard are assigned to work alongside me. My inclination is to work on my own and ignore them. But would it be so bad to work *with* them, I wonder, to cooperate? Better than being chained up by Captain Smith again with no slop bucket nearby. I decide to give it a try.

I see that it would be best to have one boy bend a sapling over, another boy chop it at its base with strong downward strokes, and the third boy drag the saplings into a brush pile. I clear my throat. "Do you want to work together on this?" I ask them. I explain my idea.

Richard eyes me warily. "Don't let him bend a sapling for you," he warns James. "He'll let it go and make it snap into your face."

I feel like punching Richard, but I know what *that* will get me. I stomp off to work by myself.

Over the next several days, we boys, servants, laborers, sailors, carpenters, and soldiers work as hard as mules. We set up the tents and bring all the bedding ashore from the ships. We dig up the ground and plant the seed wheat we brought with us from England. We tie string in knots to make nets and put the nets in the river to catch fish. We gather mussels, oysters, and crabs and bring them to the cook. We lug buckets of water from the river for cooking and washing and drinking. We fell some of the big trees and split the logs longways into planks, making clapboards. We load the clapboards onto the ships so they can be taken back to England to build English houses. We also dig up sassafras root to ship back to England. President Wingfield says it will sell at a very good price because it is used to make medicines. I am so tired by the end of each day that sometimes I fall into bed without bothering to take off my shoes.

The days are warm and the nights cool, with the constant sounds of insects and tree frogs lulling us to sleep. Some of the gentlemen pitch in and work hard, but most of them just take turns standing guard, their muskets ready, with slow matches smoking.

For several days it seems as if we are all alone in the Virginia wilderness. Then one day I look up from my hoeing and freeze, afraid to move or even cry out. Two native men come walking through the forest, quiet as deer. They each have a longbow slung over one shoulder.

"Halt!" shouts one of our gentlemen guards.

The Indian men keep coming, and I see our guards prepare to fire their muskets.

"*Wingapo!*" one of the native men calls out.

Wingapo? Captain Smith has told me this is their greeting, and it means "my beloved friend."

The Indians hold up baskets, showing us they have brought us something. And they both smile. They are tall, sturdy men, with broad, flat noses and wide lips. For clothing they wear only a breechcloth, like an apron, and their faces and shoulders are oiled with something that gives their skin a deep reddish color. Just like Richard heard from the sailors, their hair, jet black, is shaved close on the right side of their heads and grows long past their shoulders on the left side, with a ridge of short hair down the middle. The long side has decorations: One man has shells, and the other has the whole wing of a bird dangling from his hair.

Our guards approach them, still carrying their muskets. The taller of the two Indians points to the muskets, then to his longbow. He lays his bow on the ground, motioning to our guards to do the same. I see the gentlemen hesitate, but then they lay down their arms.

We gather around the baskets and find ripe red strawberries, purple mulberries, and round loaves of bread made from some kind of coarse meal. It all smells wonderful.

Captain Smith joins us and begins to converse with the men, using his hands and words from their language. He gives them glass beads and copper in return for the food they have brought.

One of the native men sees me eyeing the bread, and he laughs. He breaks a piece off, hands it to me, and nods as if saying, "Go ahead, eat it."

I say, "Thank you," even though I know he doesn't understand. The bread is delicious.

After that, the natives come to us nearly every day, sometimes two men, sometimes three. They call out "*Wingapo!*" when they approach our settlement, and always bring us baskets of food.

The natives are happy with the glass beads and copper we give them. Captain Smith explains to me how copper is rare and precious to them, so it is like gold is to the English. And they have no means to make glass, and so the beads, with their bright colors, are to them like rubies, emeralds, and diamonds are to the English. At first I thought that the Indians were strange to be willing to trade so much food for a few glass beads. But now I see that it is as if they are trading strawberries for rubies and corn for diamonds.

One day Captain Smith surprises us. "I believe the savages are spying on us," he says. "I have watched the way they look around while they are here. I think they are counting our men, seeing where our tents are located, and plotting an attack. We have invaded their land, and I believe they will fight us to get it back. We must build a palisade to protect the settlement."

"Nonsense," declares President Wingfield. "You see how friendly they are. If we build a palisade it will look as if we are their enemies. We will build no fortification."

Captain Smith grumbles, but there is no arguing with President Wingfield. And I think that President Wingfield is right; the Indians have been very friendly and welcoming to us.

Captain Smith's suspicion runs like poison through the settlement. What if the natives *are* spying on us? What if they are planning an attack? How will we protect ourselves, with no palisades?

The Virginia Company has provided our men with extra weapons and armor. In England, commoners do not carry weapons, but here almost everyone has them. Still, when the weapons and armor were being issued, by the time they got to the last of the laborers and servants, they ran out. Some of us have no protection at all.

Those who have armor begin wearing it all day, even

when it is hot. Anyone who has a sword or a musket keeps it at his side. Those of us who have no weapons discuss the merits of protective techniques, like hiding under a mattress.

"Their arrows will go right through a mattress, you fool."

"No they won't. The straw will stop them."

"Yes they *will* go right through."

"Won't."

"Will."

And so on.

On a day filled with bright, hot sunshine, I am digging up a plot, getting it ready to plant more wheat. James arrives with two buckets of water hanging from either end of a yoke balanced across his shoulders. He lowers the yoke and sets the buckets on the ground so I can drink. I take a ladle full, then spit it out. "It's *salty*," I complain. I glare at him. Has he done this on purpose, just to spite me?

But he flinches as if I might hit him, and I see the innocent look in his eyes. "High tide," he says quickly. "It hasn't rained for a while, and the river mixes with the seawater when the tide is up. It'll be better when the tide goes out. Or if it rains. That's what Master Percy said."

I take another swallow of the salty water, but it only makes me more thirsty. "Take it away," I say angrily.

James slinks off.

Reverend Hunt has seen our interaction. He comes over to talk to me. "Samuel, that poor child is unwanted by his father and despised by his stepmother. You should be able to find more kindness in your heart for him."

I hang my head. I know Reverend Hunt is right. But I have been too tired and too thirsty to think about being kind.

That night in our tent there is more discussion about an Indian attack. Henry and Abram talk of making armor for themselves out of wood. Richard and James discuss what they will do if an attack comes.

"I'm going to run to the ships," says James. "I'll row the longboat out to the *Susan Constant* and hide in the 'tween deck. No arrows can get me there."

You are a stupid, stupid boy, I think. I picture him running toward the ships, with arrows flying all around, and him with no armor. But I don't mock him or tell him he is stupid. I hope Reverend Hunt would appreciate my effort to be more kind.

Ten

The people in all places kindly entreating us, dancing, and feasting us with strawberries, mulberries, bread, fish, and other their country provisions, whereof we had plenty, for which Captain Newport kindly requited their least favors with bells, pins, needles, beads, or glasses, which so contented them that his liberality made them follow us from place to place, and ever kindly to respect us.

—Captain John Smith, *A True Relation of Such Occurrences and Accidents of Note as Hath Appeared in Virginia*

CAPTAIN NEWPORT GOES off exploring with eight or nine gentlemen and a dozen sailors. They leave in the shallop, the small boat they put together here in Virginia, so they will be able to navigate the narrow riverways. He takes Captain Smith along to be an interpreter with the Indians.

They go in search of gold and silver, and to find that new passage to the Orient everyone is talking about. They don't take many provisions with them. They say the last time they went exploring, each time they approached a village, the natives invited them in and fed them like kings.

In James Town we continue to work. We build a chapel for Reverend Hunt. We hang an old sail between four trees as an awning to protect us from sun and rain, and nail a bar between two trees for the pulpit. The walls are rails of wood that let the sunlight right in, and logs on the ground are our pews. Reverend Hunt calls us together for prayer, to thank the Almighty for all that we have, and to ask for protection.

It still has not rained, and our wheat fields and gardens are wilting. We have found no freshwater springs nearby, and so we are still dependent on the river for water. Richard, James, and I spend the afternoon bringing buckets of water from the river to dump on the tiny new shoots. When I take a drink, I find it is still salty, and I wonder if we are killing the young plants rather than saving them.

Richard and James keep to themselves, talking to each other but not to me. I think about what Reverend Hunt said about being kinder to James. But if they treat me as if I am not there, how can I be nicer? Maybe not yelling at them, not calling them names, not hitting them—maybe that is enough.

After supper there is evening prayer in the new chapel. Reverend Hunt says we will have common prayer every morning and evening from now on, and two sermons on Sundays.

By dusk I am so tired I can hardly wait to get to bed. It is cloudy—there will be no moon tonight. I go off into the woods to relieve myself. I hear a rustling nearby and squint in the half-light, but see nothing. Was it a deer? Maybe just a squirrel or a rabbit. As I walk back to camp, I hear the sound again and whip around. This time I see a form, something dark, slip behind a tree. The hair on the back of my neck bristles. But maybe it is just one of the other men, relieving himself as well.

"Who's there?" I call.

No answer.

I take a few steps toward the tree where the dark form slipped away. "*Wingapo*," I call out.

Silence.

It must have been a deer, I think. I go back to our camp.

I creep into our tent and flop onto our bed. It is the same bed that the three of us shared on the ship, and by now the straw is rotting. Henry and Abram's bed is crammed into our small tent as well, but the two of them are still out playing cards with the sailors. Richard is already asleep, dead to the world, snoring softly. James stirs, and I know he is still awake. I think about saying good night to him in an effort to be more kind. But I am so tired, I just close my eyes and am almost instantly asleep.

It drags me up out of a dream: a shriek like a demon's cry. At first I think I am still dreaming. But there is another piercing cry, then another, and soon the forest is ringing with the noise, as if all of the demons in hell have entered our camp.

I bolt upright. I can see barely more than shadows. An arrow pierces our tent and lodges in the ground next to me. James is sitting up. Richard lies there, sprawled. Has he already been shot?

"Get under the mattress—both of you!" I shout. Are they still enough afraid of me to obey?

"I'm going to the ships!" James cries. He crawls toward the tent flap.

"No!" I yell. I lunge after him, grab his ankle, yank him back. "Get under the mattress *now*!" I order him.

Richard groans. He is either waking up or dying.

James wriggles out of my grasp, heads toward the tent opening. I grab him, harder this time. He turns and sinks his teeth into the flesh of my arm.

"Yeeeow!" I snatch my hand back. In that split second, James is out of the tent.

Another arrow twangs past my ear. Richard is sitting up now, rubbing his eyes. I grasp the edge of our mattress, dump Richard onto the ground, then pull the mattress on top of both of us. I can hear my own breathing, the blood pumping in my ears. Will the mattresses protect us? I remember the discussion:

An arrow will fly right through a mattress, you idiot.

No it won't.

Yes it will.

Won't.

Will.

The argument rages in my own head. I expect any moment to feel the sharp pain of an arrow through my chest.

All around us I hear footsteps, shouting, that god-awful shrieking, the twang of arrows being shot, men crying out in pain. Finally I hear musket fire. *Kill them*, I think. But the twanging of arrows continues. I feel the impact as an arrow hits our mattress. I feel no pain.

"Richard, are you hit?" I shout.

Silence. Then, after a moment, "I don't think so."

I want to yell at him that this is a stupid answer—he is either in pain or he is not. But if I am ever going to be nicer to James and Richard, now is the time. "Do you *hurt* anywhere?" I ask.

He moves, as if he is testing his body. "No," he says.

Suddenly there is a great boom. Someone has boarded one of the ships and is shooting the cannons! I hear a crackling and a crash—the cannonball hitting a tree. Then I hear the pounding of bare feet in retreat.

Soon all is quiet. *If someone made it to the ships safely, James could be there as well*, I think.

I feel sweaty and clammy under the mattress. "I think we can come out now," I say to Richard. We both heave the mattress off of us.

Outside, men come around with torches, calling out, "Who is wounded? Who is shot?"

We crawl out of the tent and find Abram lying there, an arrow in his side. "I was just coming to bed," he says in a weak voice. "I guess I didn't quite make it."

"Here," I call out. "A man is wounded here."

Two men come and lift Abram. He groans. "We'll get you to the doctor," they say.

"James . . . he went to the ships," I tell Richard. We make our way down toward the riverbank, where our ships are moored. Along the way we step over arrows lying everywhere on the ground.

Captain Gosnold comes walking up from the river. I realize he must be the one who fired the cannon. He is carrying something draped over his outstretched arms. In the gloom of the cloudy night I can't see what it is.

I hear running footsteps behind us. "Captain," a man calls out, "there are seventeen wounded, no one dead." The running man holds a torch, and as he comes closer the torchlight glints off of Captain Gosnold's armor and makes clear what he has in his arms. It is James, his thin body lying limp.

"No," says Captain Gosnold gravely. "This one is dead."

Eleven

Hereupon the president was contented the fort should be palisadoed, the ordnance mounted, his men armed and exercised.

—William Symonds, ed., *The Proceedings*

REVEREND HUNT KNEELS with me in the dirt in front of the altar. He puts words to the prayers I cannot speak: "Please take James's soul into heaven with You, because he was just an innocent child." Then he lays a hand on my shoulder. "Samuel," he says, "you've been here a long time. Have you finished your prayers yet?"

I shake my head. How can I finish praying for forgiveness? "It was my fault," I say. My throat feels dry as sand. *I should have explained to him the danger of running to the ships. I should have been kinder to him so that he would trust me. I should have been able to grab him and pull him back into the tent. I should not have let go when he bit me. I had so many chances to keep James safe, and I failed at all of them.*

Reverend Hunt stands and reaches down a hand to pull me up. I take his hand reluctantly and rise. He looks into my eyes. "When Our Lord spoke of forgiveness he did not only mean forgiving others. Sometimes we have to forgive ourselves."

I swallow past a lump in my throat.

"Now, go wash your face and see if there is any breakfast left. You won't be able to work if you don't eat." Reverend Hunt gives me a little push, and I leave the chapel.

I trudge through the work of the day: sewing up holes in tents and mattresses, bringing water and food to our makeshift hospital where Dr. Wotton tends to the wounded men, dumping more water on our wilting plants.

Richard's eyes are red and swollen. I don't know what to say to him to make it any better. I don't think he wants to hear from me anyway. I wonder if Richard will ever forgive me, for my meanness to James while he was alive, and my failure to save him.

That afternoon Captain Smith, Captain Newport, and their party return. They say their Indian guide had acted strangely; he left them suddenly with no explanation. This made them suspicious that a raid was being planned, and so they sailed back to us as quickly as they could. They are dismayed to find that they were right.

In the evening the council calls a meeting to discuss our situation. I creep near the cabin where the council members are talking so that I can eavesdrop.

"These are not just disorganized people living in towns here and there," says Captain Newport. "They are tribes within an empire. Their emperor is called the Powhatan, the people are the Powhatans, and the river we named the James River, they already call the Powhatan River. They are a kingdom of warriors. The boys are taught to use bow and arrow when they are six years old. Their mothers don't even give them breakfast until they have shot their targets in the morning. When the great Chief Powhatan wants to conquer a new tribe, the warriors get the job done very quickly."

"There's a prophecy they told us about," says Master Percy. "The bay we first entered on our way here they call the Chesapeake Bay. There used to be a tribe, the Chesapeakes, living on its shores. The prophecy says that a threat to Chief Powhatan's empire will come from the Chesapeake Bay. When he heard this, he sent his warriors and in one day they wiped out the Chesapeake tribe."

"There must have been four hundred of them last night," says Captain Gosnold. "If it had not been for the cannons scaring them off, they would have easily killed us all."

There is silence then. *No one wants to tell President Wingfield that he was wrong and Captain Smith was right about building a palisade*, I think. President Wingfield, to his credit, had been at the forefront of the battle. Those who saw him said that he fired his musket even as an arrow went right through his beard. I hold my breath. *Please, someone tell him we need to build a strong fort!*

"All right." President Wingfield's voice breaks the silence. "There will be watches, armed men at every corner in shifts throughout the day and night. And"—he hesitates a moment—"tomorrow we will begin construction of a tall palisade, with not so much as a crack between the posts."

I let out my breath and creep away before anyone catches me listening.

FEAR MAKES US work fast. We fell trees and make them into palisade posts with wickedly sharp tips. We dig a trench in a large triangle around our tents and plant our posts so close together an arrow cannot get through. Each corner of the triangle is rounded like a half-moon, with a platform inside. We bring cannons from the ships and mount them on the platforms. We are making a fort, like soldiers in a war.

Thank goodness the sailors are still with us. They, along with our laborers, soldiers, and other working men, are the ones with the strength and speed to get the job done. If we had to depend on the gentlemen, many of whom still don't want to dirty their velvet, we would be at the mercy of the Indians for many more weeks. As it is, the natives mount small attacks every other day on any man or creature who strays too far from our guarded, half-built fort.

They shoot Master Clovell while he is out hunting. He comes running back to the fort with arrows sticking out of him and dies soon after. They shoot and kill another man in the woods when he drops his slops to relieve himself. They even shoot one of Captain Newport's dogs while she is sniffing after a rabbit.

Captain Smith finds me using a hatchet to sharpen palisade post tips. He is holding a belt, sheath, sword, and armor. I recognize the sword—it has a *C* molded into the handle. It belonged to Master Clovell, whose grave I just helped to dig.

"Samuel, do you think you can put some of that energy from your fistfights into learning to use a sword?" Captain Smith asks.

My hatchet stops in midair. "Yes, sir," I say. I try not to sound too eager.

"You are, after all, apprentice to an officer," he says. "It is time to begin your training."

I lay my tools on the ground and wipe my hands on my slops.

"You're lucky," Captain Smith says. "Master Clovell was a slight man. His belt and armor will fit you well."

And they won't fit Henry or Abram or any of the other

unarmed men who want them, I think. With arrows flying every day, weapons and armor are more coveted than gold.

"Captain, you're not taking my worker, are you?" John Laydon asks. He is the carpenter overseeing the building of the palisades.

"I'd better take him now and teach him a thing or two so he'll live to work another day," Captain Smith says.

John Laydon nods, and I've got permission to leave.

Master Clovell's armor is a little bit big, but it fits well enough. I will grow into it. The breastplate makes me feel like I have a large chest. I rap my knuckles on it and admire the clang. No arrow can pierce this metal. The helmet is heavy. I feel like a soldier already.

"Will I have a musket, too?" I ask.

"First you will learn to use a sword," Captain Smith says.

I fasten the belt around my waist and pull the sword out of its sheath. The handle is smooth and cool, and the sword is heavy. It glints in the sun. I take it in both hands and whip it through the air. It makes a sharp *whoosh.*

Captain Smith begins my instruction. I want to think about the sword, but he tells me I must think about my feet, and watch his feet as well. It is like dancing, he says. But I have never learned to dance, and so it is all new.

"It is a dance of death with your opponent," he says. "You mirror his steps until you see a weak spot—and then you *lunge.*" He suddenly steps forward, knee bent, and I am stuck in the chest with his blade. I gasp and look down.

Captain Smith laughs at my terrified expression. "Did you forget you were wearing armor?"

I let my breath out in a rush. "No," I lie.

"You must block me; don't let me enter your circle." Slowly, he goes again for a lunge.

I think fast, swat his sword with my blade, knock his off of its course toward my chest.

"Very good!" he shouts.

We pattern our steps as in a slow dance, him giving me time to balance his movements with my own. He raises his eyebrows when he is about to strike, his signal to me to protect myself. I hear the satisfying clang as my sword knocks his away.

We speed up, our feet moving more and more quickly. No time for thought now, only reaction. I am out of breath, sweating, our swords clanging, ringing out. He is always one step ahead of me, always quicker. I am tiring. Then I see a gap—my chance to enter his circle. I step forward, *lunge*. Suddenly there is a scraping, a pain in my hand, and my sword is wrenched from my grasp. It lands on the ground behind me, and I stand there, unarmed, with Captain Smith's sword hovering just in front of my throat.

I am defeated.

But Captain Smith laughs. "It takes a long time to learn to use a sword properly, Samuel. Go pick it up."

I rub my sore fingers and move them until they feel better. Then I grasp the sword again, narrow my eyes, and concentrate. I will try again.

Captain Smith moves slowly at first, giving me a chance to find my rhythm. Then he speeds up as before, and I follow. I put my mind aside and feel only my body, stepping, moving. The dance of death sweeps us into its circle. Our swords clash and clang. My breath comes in short gasps. I see the opening. I *lunge*.

My blade finds its mark. The tip presses into Captain Smith's armor, just above his heart. He holds up his hands, drops his sword. He speaks slowly. "The student," he says gravely, "has impaled the teacher."

I begin to shake my head. I did not mean to anger him.

Then he breaks into a broad smile.

I wipe beads of sweat from my face. My hand is shaking.

"We will train every day," he tells me. "Wear your armor whenever you leave the fort. The sword will be no match for flying arrows, but tomorrow I will begin to teach you to use another weapon—one that is much more powerful than this sword."

I nod calmly, but inside I am excited. Tomorrow I will learn to use a *musket*.

Twelve

Wingapo: Hello (literally, "My beloved friend")
Pokatawer: Fire
Attonce: Arrows
Netoppew: Friends
Marrapough: Enemies
Werowance: Chief (literally, "He is wealthy")

–From Algonquian/English word lists compiled by
Thomas Harriot, John Smith, and William Strachey

THE NEXT MORNING, Captain Smith does not bring me a musket. He brings me a book. It is well worn and the stitching is coming loose. I sound out the letters of two of the words on the cover: "Thomas Harriot."

"Thomas Harriot lived in the Roanoke colony," Captain Smith explains. "He learned much of the Algonquian language, wrote it down, brought his papers back to England, and they were published in this book. I want you to learn these words. They will be better protection than any weapon."

I open the book. The pages hold two columns. On the left are words I understand: *man, houses, shoes, axe, sea turtle*. On the right are strange words I've never seen before: *nemarough, yehawkans, moccasins, tomahawk, terrapin*. Farther down the page is a word with no English translation next to it. I sound it out. "*Raccoon*," I say. "What does that mean?"

"It's an animal we don't have in England," he says. "You'll see one soon enough, especially if you're out at night. It's a bit like a small badger, with black circles around its eyes."

"*Raccoon*," I say again, trying to imagine such an animal. I find numbers: one, two, three is translated *necut, ningh, nuss*.

"This language will be your protection outside the fort, and within it as well," he says. I know he means that this will make me valuable as a translator to the gentlemen who might have little use for me otherwise.

I am disappointed that I won't be learning to use a musket. But the new words roll off my tongue and make me feel as if there is power in them.

And so every day we drill. Just like the young Powhatan boys who don't get their breakfast until they have shot their targets, I do not get my breakfast until I have done a bit of sword fighting and learned at least two new words in Algonquian.

IN JUNE, CAPTAIN Smith's name is finally cleared, and he is sworn in on the council. Maybe it is because he has been too busy lately to insult the gentlemen every single day, or because Reverend Hunt has interceded for him yet again, or simply because the council members see that they need his good sense and important skills. At last, Captain Smith has been given the position that the Virginia Company assigned to him.

On June 22, Captain Newport and the rest of the mariners set sail for England. They carry loads of clapboard and sassafras root, and barrels of shiny rocks that we hope contain gold. They sail away in the *Susan Constant* and the *Godspeed* and leave the *Discovery* and the shallop for us to use for travel here in Virginia. Captain Newport also takes all of the food stores except fourteen weeks' worth of wheat and barley for the one hundred or so of us colonists. He says he will return with fresh stores by October.

IT BEGINS A FEW days after Captain Newport leaves. First one man, then another, then five more, then a dozen, all groaning and feverish with swollen faces and bloody diarrhea. Never have I heard such sounds of misery: the moaning and whimpering, the begging to be released from their bodies. And then they begin to be released, sometimes one, sometimes two or three, turning

EDISON JR. HIGH LEARNING CTR

up stiff and cold in the morning. I feel dizzy and nauseated, but I am still able to stand, and so I help to drag the bodies outside the fort and dig graves.

Soon there are so many sick that there is no one with strength to tend the gardens, no one with strength to hunt or fish. We are left with a cup of barley and a cup of wheat for each man per day, and this is filled with wriggling mealworms. I help cook the grains in the big pot over our communal cook fire, and I watch as the mealworms float to the top.

As we grow hungrier, more and more men become ill. Those who still have the energy to argue have theories about what is causing the sickness.

"It's a curse. The savages have cursed us," one man says.

"No, you're wrong. It's the filthy river water," says another. "It's salty at high tide and slimy at low tide, and it's all we've got to drink."

"You're both wrong. It's starvation, pure and simple," comes another explanation. "There's more worms than grain in our meal."

"No, no, no. It's the wet and chill that's killing us. The rain comes right into my tent and I sleep shivering every night."

"Sleep? Who gets to sleep? I'm on watch every third night. A man can't stay healthy when he gets no rest."

"You're all wrong," says yet another. "It's ratsbane.

There's a Spanish spy among us, and he is poisoning us all! I know arsenic poisoning when I see it."

But soon, even those who think they have an explanation are too sick for discussions. Captain Smith falls ill. Then Captain Gosnold and Master Percy. Then Richard, too. And Reverend Hunt.

Some days I cannot stand. I lie in my bed, groaning from the pain in my belly. Whether it is from hunger, poison, or sickness, all I know is that I am miserable.

On the days when I can move, I bring food and water to Captain Smith, Reverend Hunt, and Richard. They are all sicker than I. Richard just looks at me when I bring him the salty water and wormy grain. I wonder if he thinks I am bringing him such bad fare out of spite, and not because it is all we have. His eyes are glassy, with a faraway look. I think he will likely die even before the two of us have had a chance to put the past behind us and become friends.

Henry is still up and around, doing his chores for President Wingfield, but Abram is ill. President Wingfield himself is in the finest of health.

I hear Henry and Abram whispering one night when they think I am asleep.

"I stole an egg for you. You'll have to eat it raw," says Henry.

I hear the cracking of eggshell and loud slurping.

"I'll get you some wine tomorrow. Meat, too. I told

him if he doesn't share the stores with you and me, he'll be doing his own laundry and mending soon."

I suck in my breath. They've got *eggs*? We ate all our chickens weeks ago, and shared the last eggs all around. At least we *thought* those were the last eggs.

"What's that?" Henry's voice startles me. "You're awake, then, you scum?"

Suddenly his thick hand is at my throat and his dark form looms over me. "You heard nothing, do you understand me?" he hisses. We are very close to the other tents so he speaks softly, but with cold meanness. "*Nothing.*"

I try to nod, but his hand clamps harder on my throat. I can't breathe.

"Swear it," he demands. "Swear in God's name you will tell no one what you heard."

"I swear it," I croak.

He gives my throat one last shake, then releases me.

"Speak of it and you will die," he says. I have no doubt he means it.

He is protecting his master. Without his master, Henry may be of no use to anyone. He might not even be worth his share of the dwindling food rations. He is protecting himself.

I lie in the dark, listening to Richard's ragged breathing. Will he die with his last memory of me being of something mean I said or did to him? And what of Captain

Smith and Reverend Hunt? Will they die and leave me with no one to be my ally against the anger and whims of the gentlemen, or of Henry?

The next morning, two more corpses are dragged out of the tents. I am barely able to stand, but I will help to dig the graves. In my head I count up how many of us there are left and realize we have buried half our men.

"The savages might as well come finish us off now," I hear a man say. "And we'll disappear just like the Roanoke colony did."

And all the while Master Wingfield eats his meat and drinks his wine.

John Laydon brings two shovels, one for me and one for him. We don't go far from the fort to dig the graves. Two soldiers come with us as guards. As we dig, we look warily around, hoping there are no Indians to shoot at us today. If we had more strength, and more courage, we could go into the forest to hunt and bring back fresh meat. But too many men have gone to hunt and have staggered back into the fort with arrows in their bellies, only to die in agony a few days later.

And now I know: There is meat and eggs within the walls of our fort.

Captain Smith is looking a little better today—he is up on his own, and so I will not need to bring him breakfast. I bring a bowl of wormy grains to Reverend Hunt in his tent. He is pale and lean, his cheeks sunken in.

When I hand him the bowl, he fumbles with it and nearly drops it. Can he live much longer on this foul food and salty water?

"Reverend Hunt, I have a question," I say.

He nods. He is ready to listen.

"If I have sworn not to do something—sworn in God's name—must I keep my word?"

He frowns. "Who has made you swear something in God's name?" he demands.

I hang my head. I cannot tell this, or Henry will clamp his hand around my throat until there is no breath left in me.

Reverend Hunt's hand shakes as he lifts a spoonful of gruel to his mouth. He chews, thinking, then speaks. "If you will not tell me all of it, I cannot give you an answer. But you are capable of finding the answer on your own. Your heart will know better than your head. Choose the path of love and not of fear. The choice you make out of love will always be the right one."

I leave him and go to chop wood for the cook fire. With the last of my strength I slam my frustration into the wood with my axe. I hate Henry. I hate being afraid of him. If I keep my sworn oath to him, is that a choice made out of love? No. It is a choice made out of fear. Have I grown to love Reverend Hunt, with his patience and wisdom and his love for me? *Yes*.

I throw down the axe. I have made my decision. I will

tell what I have sworn not to tell. I go to find Captain Smith where he is helping John Laydon to split clapboard. They are both weak and the work is going slowly.

"Captain Smith," I say, "I would like to speak to you—in private."

Thirteen

As I understand by report I am much charged with starving the colony, I did always give every man his allowance faithfully, both of corn, oil, aqua vitae, etc., as was by the council proportioned.

–Edward Maria Wingfield, *A Discourse of Virginia*

MASTER WINGFIELD IS no longer our president. He is under arrest, locked up on the *Discovery*, and his private store of wine, dried beef, eggs, oatmeal, and other good food has been shared equally among all of us. He says he was keeping it to dole out to us if we ran out of provisions, but that didn't keep the council from voting him down. Now we have Captain Ratcliffe as our president. Captain Smith says we have gone from the frying pan into the fire.

Reverend Hunt is looking much better. Many of us

gave him some of our share of eggs and meat, and so he has been eating well for days. We have had rain, too—great drenching storms of it. We have caught it in buckets and barrels to drink, and the river is no longer so salty. The rainwater tastes so sweet, I would think it had honey in it. Reverend Hunt has color in his cheeks again, and he is able to lead Sunday services for the first time in many weeks.

Captain Smith has taken all of the credit for discovering Master Wingfield's stash, and for that I am grateful. Henry has no idea it was I who told, and so he has had no compulsion to kill me.

Richard is much better now, too. I am relieved. I decide to take the first step toward becoming his friend.

"Richard, you want to see my sword?" I ask one day when he is up and looking stronger. "I could show you some of what Captain Smith is teaching me."

Richard looks at me warily, as if he thinks this could be a trick.

"I just thought you might be interested," I say quietly. I look down, avoiding his eyes.

There is silence between us. Then Richard says, "Are you ready to fight a duel yet?"

I cringe. Is he challenging me to a duel? But when I look up he is grinning.

"Not yet," I tell him, "but Captain Smith says I'm learning well. Come on, I'll show you a few things."

I let Richard try on my armor and have him fasten the belt around his waist so he can feel the weight of the sword, too. He pulls the sword out of its sheath and holds it in both hands. I tell him about what Captain Smith is teaching me: the footwork, and the sword work.

Suddenly Richard closes his eyes and a look of pure sadness comes across his face.

"Richard, what is it? Are you going to faint?" I never should have had him try on heavy armor when he is barely well.

He shakes his head. "James," he says. "If—" He stops himself to keep from crying.

"I know," I say. "I've thought about it a hundred times. If only James had had armor, he might still be alive."

Richard nods, grateful that I have said what he was thinking.

Then a thought strikes me. "Richard, *you* need armor. So many have died, there must be extra. Let's go talk to Captain Smith."

Together we go to Captain Smith to ask. He takes a good look at Richard. He is a couple of inches shorter than I am and somewhat wider. Captain Smith scratches his beard, thinking. "No one as slight as Master Clovell has died . . . but we will cut some armor down to fit you."

The blacksmith is put to work to remake a chest-plate. The first time Richard stands wearing his armor, he grins at me. I know I am on my way to making a friend.

Captain Smith decides that now that some of us are well, every able-bodied man must be skilled at using a musket. He gathers the men who are new to weapons—the commoners and servants—to begin training.

He shows us how to keep the slow match burning by blowing the ash off of it every few minutes, and how to use it to ignite the gunpowder. We learn each step: prime the pan, charge the piece with powder, put in the musket ball, ram down the charge, cock the match. . . .

We use a big tree with a mark on it as a target. The first time I fire my musket the kick nearly throws me onto the ground. I miss the tree completely, but so do most of the others.

By the end of our training session my ears are ringing, my arms are sore, and I smell like gunpowder, but I have hit the mark three times. Captain Smith says we will continue to train each week until that tree is full of musket shot.

The extra rations from Master Wingfield do not last long, and soon we are back to the wormy grains. I wonder why the natives do not mount another raid if they really want us gone. There are hardly fifty of us left, and those that are left are half starved and weak.

Maybe they're just letting starvation finish us off, I think. Outside the fort is plenty of food: fish, oysters, rabbits, berries. But there are also Indians hiding behind the trees. No one has the courage to venture out any farther than is necessary to dig the graves for our dead.

Then one day I hear the words I've been dreading. "Savages!" "Arm yourselves!" "We're under attack!"

I hear the scraping of metal as the guards load the cannons. *This is it*, I think. *They've been watching, waiting, maybe even counting our burials. They know we have only a few men left. They've come to wipe out our colony.*

Richard and I hurry to put on our armor and ready our muskets. Soon we hear shouts from outside the fort. But these are not the shrill battle cries I have expected any moment. They are calls of "*Wingapo!*"

Richard and I run to the front gates of the fort. The gates have been thrown wide open, and natives—men, women, and children—are walking in. They look around curiously at our rotting tents and the big iron pot hanging over the cook fire. They all carry baskets. When I see what is in the baskets I gasp. They are filled with bread, corn, fish, meat, squash, and berries. The smell of the fresh bread makes me nearly faint with hunger.

One of our soldiers tries to grab a chunk of meat right out of a basket, but the Indian man holding it puts up his hand abruptly to stop him. Captain Smith comes forward. He speaks in Algonquian with our visitors, and I listen closely, trying to understand what they are saying: They are here to trade. They will give us food from their recent harvest in exchange for our copper, hatchets, swords, and muskets. Captain Smith nods agreeably. I wonder if he will actually give them swords and muskets. The Virginia Company has given us strict orders never to let the Indians get their hands on our weapons.

Captain Smith translates for our leaders. Our visitors say that within the Powhatan empire, there are tribes who are our friends, and some who are our enemies. Our enemies are the tribes closest to us because they feel we are encroaching on their land. They are the Paspahegh, whose land we are on, and also the Weanock, the Appamatuck, the Kiskiack, and the Quiyoughcohanock. Our friends are the Arrohateck, the Pamunkey, the Mattaponi, and the Youghtanund. Those who are our friends will intercede for us with our enemies. They will try to convince them that we pose no threat, that we are only using a small piece of land, and we are not making war with them. They also tell us we should cut down the tall grass near our fort, because that is where our enemies are hiding when they shoot at us.

Captain Smith tells them we are thankful for their message, and for their peacekeeping efforts. Then he invites them to come sit in our common eating area around our fire pit. We all watch hungrily as they negotiate the trading. Captain Smith drives a hard bargain; he will not give away a single bead cheaply.

By the time the Indians leave, all of the baskets of food have become ours. They leave with some colorful glass beads, mirrors, bells, needles, pins, several pieces of copper, and three hatchets. Captain Smith does not trade away a single sword or musket.

Fourteen

The new president . . . committed the managing of all things abroad to Captain Smith, who by his own example, good words, and fair promises set some to mow, others to bind thatch, some to build houses, others to thatch them, himself always bearing the greatest task for his own share.

—William Symonds, ed., *The Proceedings*

CAPTAIN NEWPORT DOES not return in October with new supplies. But instead of being hungrier, we have finally gotten through the sickness and we are healthy again. The tribes who are our friends must have convinced our enemies to stop attacking us, and it is no longer dangerous to leave the fort to hunt or fish. We have a pitiful harvest of wheat and vegetables from our gardens, but the Indians often bring us food from their own harvests to trade.

The air is filled with birds flying south for the winter,

and it is easy to shoot enough for a meal. We have more rain, and the river water is good to drink.

Captain Smith has been put in charge of trading with the Indians. If we ever run short of corn or meat, he takes a few men, and some beads and copper for trading, and sails off in the shallop for a few days to visit some of the Indian villages. They always come back with the shallop full of supplies.

Captain Smith is also in charge of getting houses built for all of us. With the weather turning colder we can't keep sleeping in our rotting tents. He sets for us the goal of houses for everyone and cheers us on, exhorting us to push ahead. We work hard together, Captain Smith always working the hardest, with some felling trees, some splitting wood for clapboard, some cutting reeds for thatch. We use shaped timbers to frame the houses, and the carpenters teach us how to weave sticks together to make a mesh, then coat the mesh with a mixture of river clay and straw to make wattle and daub walls. We bundle the reeds to make thatched roofs. I have never helped to build a house before, and it makes me proud to see my work. I see what Captain Smith meant about us needing to stand on many legs to survive. We have to work together. I would never be able to build a house all by myself.

Some of the gentlemen work hard with us, too, until their hands are rough as commoners' hands. By the time the weather turns cold, we have put up warm, dry houses for everyone, even the servants.

In early December, Captain Smith chooses nine men to sail with him in the shallop up the Chickahominy River. They are hoping to find the passage to the Pacific Ocean and the Orient, and they think the Chickahominy might lead to it.

When I ask Captain Smith why this passage to the Pacific is so important, he explains it to me. "The nobles in England want spices and silks and ivory. The best place to get them is the Orient—China and India. Between England and the Orient going east over land, are the Ottoman Turks. The Turks gladly sell us all the Chinese silks and Indian spices we want. They buy it for tuppence and then sell it to England for bags of gold. If we can find a way to the Orient over the ocean going *west*, we can skip the Turks altogether, and that would make the Virginia Company investors very happy, and *very* rich."

Captain Smith and his men leave on a frosty morning, and we all wish them well. Once Captain Smith is gone, though, the gentlemen stop working and even the common men shirk their chores. If it wasn't for us servants, the food wouldn't get cooked, the water wouldn't get toted, and the wood wouldn't get chopped for the fires.

One cold morning in mid-December, Richard and I are working with the embers that are all that is left of our cabin's fire, trying to bring them to flame. Richard sprinkles dry moss on the embers, and I blow on them softly. At the first hint of flame, we add twigs. It feels good to be cooperating with Richard, to be his friend.

"Come on, fire," Richard coaxes.

I rub my hands together to warm them. It was Abram and Henry's turn to feed the fire during the night but they, just like everyone else, don't think much of chores these days.

The twigs catch, we add some bigger chips of wood, keep blowing, and soon we have a good fire going. I cough on the smoke. We don't have a proper hearth with a chimney like Mum and I used to have in our cottage. This is just a circle of stones on our dirt floor, and to let the smoke out, there is a hole at the top of the eaves. Our cabin is always smoky—it doesn't even have any windows—and it has begun to leak in heavy rains, but it is still a lot better than a rotting tent.

Within minutes there is a voice at the door. "We need an ember," comes the demand.

Richard and I look at each other. Every morning it is the same. As soon as anyone sees smoke coming from our cabin, they come for embers, because they all let their fires go completely out during the night.

I open the door and find Master Crofts dressed in his thick wool cassock, but looking rather blue-lipped from the cold. I take his spoon, fish out an ember from our fire, and send him on his way. He doesn't even thank me.

"I think they'd freeze if they didn't have us around," I say.

"And starve," says Richard.

Next comes Master Houlgrave, then Master Frith, then Nathaniel, who has become a soldier, asking for an ember for the soldiers' cabin.

"Look how disciplined our soldiers are," Richard says after Nathaniel leaves.

Richard puts an ember into a pan to take to Reverend Hunt in case his fire, too, has gone out. I go to see if anyone has bothered to start the hominy in the big communal cook pot.

I hear one of the guards call out, "It is the shallop returned! Hello, explorers! Have you found the passage to India?"

Captain Smith must be back! I rush to the fort gates. Six men come trailing in. They are tired, dragging their muskets as they walk. There is not a smile among them. And Captain Smith is not with them.

They come to the communal cook fire to warm themselves. There, Abram is stirring the big pot of hominy, a porridge we make from coarse ground corn. The rest of us gather around. We listen as they give their report. The river became too narrow to explore with the shallop. Captain Smith went off with two men, Jehu Robinson and Thomas Emry, to find an Indian guide and a canoe. He did not return. Indians captured one of their men, George

Cassen. The last they saw of him, he was tied to a stake with a fire being built around him. They were glad to escape with their lives.

I listen, my heart sinking lower and lower. Has Captain Smith been captured by the Indians as well? Has he, too, been killed?

Abram scoops the hominy into the mess pots, but I don't want to eat. I leave the fort and go down to the riverbank. There was hoar frost last night, and all of the bare branches are coated white and sparkling. I walk along the river a little way, then sit down on a jumble of tree roots and look out across the dark water. What will happen to me now? I have seen how Henry and Abram have been treated since Master Wingfield was put under arrest. It is as if they were suddenly declared every gentleman's servant, always washing this one's stockings, fetching that one's firewood. President Ratcliffe sometimes puts them on double watch shifts, so that they get no rest, and they go around red-eyed and bad-tempered. But being overworked would not be the worst of it. No, the worst would be losing someone I have grown to trust and care about.

I pick up a small stone and throw it sidearmed, making it skip across the water. Five skips. Richard and I should have a contest. I am suddenly very grateful that Richard is now my ally, not my enemy. Reverend Hunt, too. I am thankful that he is still with us. Without the two of them, I would have no one to care whether I live or die. In London it was easy to survive on my own, rummaging in garbage for my meals. Here it is better to have a few people to stick up for you and make sure you get your food rations. More legs to stand on, Captain Smith would say.

I hear crunching—footsteps in the frozen dead leaves covering the ground. It is Richard. He is carrying my bowl and spoon. He hands me the steaming bowl of hominy and sits next to me.

"Thank you," I say. I am very hungry now. It would have been miserable to go all day without breakfast.

He nods, wraps his arms around his knees, and rests his chin on them. "Maybe he will still come back," he says.

"Maybe."

When my bowl is empty, I pick up a flat stone. "How many skips can you do?" I ask.

Richard grins. "More than you, that's for sure."

We gather stones, and the contest is on.

THE LETTER COMES just before Christmas. Three Indian messengers bring it to the fort gates, and I rejoice to see Captain Smith's handwriting.

"I am well," the letter says. "Fire the cannons and a few rounds from your muskets to scare these fellows. And give them a handful of beads, a pound of copper, and five hatchets, which I have promised to give to the Pamunkeys."

I run to tell Reverend Hunt and Richard. "He is with the Pamunkeys!" I exclaim. "They are one of the friendly tribes."

"I see he still has his paper and quill with him," says Reverend Hunt.

"He must still be writing our story," I say, beaming.

JUST AFTER NEW YEAR 1608, Richard goes out before me to start the cook pot of hominy for our communal breakfast. He comes back not five minutes later, his face white as linen.

"It's gone," he whispers. "The corn. All of it."

"What do you mean, it's gone?" I ask. "Yesterday there was plenty. Enough for two weeks, at least."

Richard shakes his head. "I looked for the barrel of smoked meat, too. And baskets of dried oysters. Gone."

I feel the blood drain from my face. Are natives now *stealing* our food instead of bringing it to us? Or have raccoons and foxes gotten into our stores? But we had men on guard all night.

I run out of the cabin to see for myself. Richard is right—our food is gone. Then I notice something else: The fort is eerily quiet. There is hardly anyone around. The only activity is two laborers chopping firewood and a soldier sitting outside his cabin cleaning his musket. The sun is already up, and the gentlemen should have been grumbling for their breakfast. The day is quite cold, with a pale winter sun, and yet not a single gentleman has come to our cabin for an ember.

"Where are they?" I demand, fear growing in the pit of my stomach.

"Who?" Richard asks.

"The *gentlemen*."

Fifteen

Now in James Town they were all in combustion, the strongest preparing once more to run away with the pinnace for England.

—William Symonds, ed., *The Proceedings*

THE *DISCOVERY* BOBS in the river as the gentlemen on board unfurl her sails. There is no wind yet, but their intent is clear. They have loaded up all of our food, and as soon as a breeze lifts, they will set sail for England. There are ten or twelve gentlemen on board and they are leaving the twenty-five of us commoners behind to starve.

In twos and threes men come out from the fort to stare at the *Discovery*.

"I'll shoot them all," one of the soldiers declares. He prepares to load his musket.

"Don't be stupid," Henry says. "They'll shoot you before you can fire a second shot, and they'll hit some of the rest of us as well."

"They've already killed us," says John Laydon. "You think we'll make it through the winter? The river will freeze over our fishnets, the birds are already gone, and there's nothing more to harvest. We might as well be shot. At least it'll be a quick death."

My stomach grumbles for its breakfast. I wonder how long it takes to die of hunger. I wonder if it hurts.

The men continue to argue. Some think we'll be able to trade with the Indians, and others insist that the Indians will not trade now in mid-winter when they are probably going half-hungry themselves. Many want to kill the gentlemen, or die trying.

Reverend Hunt is standing near me. He is staring out at the ship, his face set in grim lines. "Is it all lost, Reverend?" I ask him. "Are we doomed?"

He puts his hand on my shoulder. "Do you see any wind?" he asks.

I take a good look at the surface of the river. There is hardly a ripple. I shake my head.

"Then the *Discovery* is not going anywhere—yet. There is time for me to pray for a miracle." He walks off in the direction of the fort, to the chapel.

I listen to the men argue about how to shoot to kill the most gentlemen at once. Richard touches my arm. His eyes are bright. "Look!" he whispers, pointing back behind us.

At first I think I am seeing a vision, that my imagination is playing tricks. I see a dozen native men emerging from the forest near the fort. Some are bare-chested despite the cold, and some have deerskin mantles thrown over one shoulder. They are walking quickly. There is one man among them who is not quite a native, though not quite a white man either. His hair is reddish-brown, but long and shaggy. He is wearing a deerskin mantle, and also slops and shoes. Suddenly it is as if my eyes clear, and I know who I am seeing.

"Captain Smith!" I cry, and run full speed to greet him.

Everyone starts clamoring at once. "They're leaving us!" "They've stolen our food." "We've no stores left." "Those no-good lazy gentlemen . . ." "We'll starve!" "Where have you *been*?"

Captain Smith holds up his hand to silence us. "Help me with the cannons," he orders. We follow him to the fort and our soldiers work to load the cannons and aim them squarely at the *Discovery*.

Then Captain Smith marches down to the water's edge. "Halt or be sunk!" he shouts. "Disembark at once, or die."

We watch as the gentlemen on board the ship huddle and talk. After a few minutes of conferring with one another, Master Archer shouts out, "Where are Jehu Robinson and Thomas Emry?"

Captain Smith shakes his head. "Dead," he answers. "Killed by the savages."

The gentlemen confer some more, and then begin to load the longboat with provisions to bring back to shore.

A cheer goes up among the commoners. Our food is being returned to us. But I have an uneasy feeling. Why did the gentlemen change their minds as soon as Captain Smith told them that those two men are dead? I watch them paddle the longboat toward shore and think it almost feels too easy, this change in their plans.

We turn our attention to Captain Smith with a hundred questions. "Where did you go?" "Why did you stay away so long?" "Did you bring corn?" "Did the Indians try to kill you?"

"Later," he says. "I will tell you all about it later."

The group of native men who have come with Captain Smith stand quietly watching as the gentlemen roll barrels of provisions up the riverbank. Once the *Discovery* has been unmanned, Captain Smith turns back toward the fort. "*Peyaquaugh*," he says to the native men.

"That means to go with him," I say to Richard.

Richard and I follow, too. Captain Smith brings the men to the fort, where two of our cannons sit perched on an artillery platform. He speaks to them in Algonquian as best he can. "Here—guns I promise to Great Powhatan. You take to him."

My jaw drops open. We are forbidden to give the Indians muskets or swords, but Captain Smith is giving them *cannons*?

The Indian men gather around one of the cannons to lift it. They strain, switch positions, team up, push and pull with all their might. Their faces turn red, veins on their necks stand out, and they sweat despite the icicles hanging from the trees. I glance over at Captain Smith and see that he is stifling a smile.

"I give something easy for carry," he offers. The would-be cannon carriers look relieved. They finally leave with handfuls of intricately colored glass beads, some bells, small mirrors, and a large copper pot. I wonder if the Great Powhatan will be satisfied with the switch.

"Now will you tell us where you've been?" John Laydon asks.

"Did you really meet the Great Powhatan?" I ask.

"Can't a man get breakfast before he has to give an oration?" Captain Smith says.

Richard and I find the half-full barrel of corn and cook up a large pot of hominy. After breakfast, we keep the common cook fire going so we can warm ourselves while Captain Smith tells his story. Most of the common men come to listen. The gentlemen are, again, nowhere to be seen. Are they off sulking like scolded dogs, I wonder? Or hatching a new plan?

But once Captain Smith begins his story, I don't give

the gentlemen another thought. "Two hundred savages came upon me," he says. "They captured me and took me prisoner. They paraded me from one village to another, and at each village there were ceremonies and dancing, with dancers painted red and black like fearsome devils. And there was feasting—lots of feasting. I was sure that as soon as I was fat enough for their liking, they would kill me and eat me."

"I thought the Powhatans were *not* cannibals," I blurt out.

Captain Smith shakes his head. "I didn't think so, but why else were they fattening me up?" He raises his eyebrows at me. "Finally I was taken to the village of Werowocomoco. I was presented to Wahunsonacock, the Great Powhatan himself. He sat on a throne covered with a large robe made of raccoon skins with the tails still on. All around him sat his court, upwards of two hundred men and women, their faces and shoulders painted red and crowns of white bird feathers on their heads. They had another feast, and then two large stones were brought and placed in front of Chief Powhatan." Captain Smith pantomimes lifting two heavy stones. "Suddenly, seven or eight warriors jumped up from their seats and seized me! They dragged me over and forced my head down on one of the stones. Three warriors stood over me with heavy clubs. They raised the clubs, ready to bash my brains out."

I suck in my breath. Henry looks at me and rolls his

eyes. "Well, he didn't *get* his brains bashed out, now did he?" he says.

I glare at Henry and go back to listening.

"There was no way for me to escape. With so many men holding me down, I could not even move," Captain Smith says. "I prepared to die."

We are silent, waiting for the next turn in the story.

"Suddenly I heard the voice of a child begging for my life to be spared. But Chief Powhatan refused the requests. He declared, 'No. The Englishman will die.'

"Then I saw who had been speaking. It was a little girl, about nine or ten years old. She came running over to me. She ignored the warriors with their raised clubs. She gathered my head in her arms, and laid her own head down over mine. The warriors could not strike a blow now without hitting her first."

We are amazed by what we have heard. After a moment Henry breaks the silence. "Aw, I don't believe it," he says. "You made it all up, you did."

Captain Smith is on his feet in a second. He catches Henry up by the front of his shirt. "That little girl has more courage than you will ever have. And don't you *ever* call me a liar again."

Henry cowers. "Yes, sir," he says.

I want the story to continue, but just then President Ratcliffe, Master Martin, Master Archer, and a few of the other gentlemen come crowding into our circle. Several of them grab Captain Smith and hold him fast. We are too stunned to do anything.

"What is going on here?" Captain Smith bellows. He thrashes at the men, but they jerk his arms behind his back, tie his hands together, and clamp chains around his ankles.

"Stop this!" John Laydon cries. He lifts his musket, but it is beaten out of his hands by Master Archer. "Watch yourself, or you'll face the gallows as well," Master Archer warns.

The *gallows*?

"You are under arrest," Master Archer announces. "The law of Leviticus states 'an eye for an eye, a tooth for a tooth, a life for a life.' You are responsible for the deaths of Thomas Emry and Jehu Robinson, as they were in your care. You will pay for those deaths with your life. Your execution will be at sunup tomorrow."

Captain Smith struggles, but he is tied so tightly hand and foot that he can hardly move. "You're mad!" he cries. "There is no English law that makes me responsible for those deaths."

But the gentlemen don't listen. They drag him away, his chains clanking.

Rage bubbles up inside me. Without thinking I snatch up a rock and hurl it straight at the back of Master Archer's head. Master Archer howls. He grabs his bleeding scalp and turns to look at us. I stand there, seething with anger.

I feel the old urges, the desire to punch and rip, to see blood before my fury is spent. Captain Smith's voice speaks in my head, *Learn to channel your anger, Samuel, and it will become your strength rather than your weakness.*

"I know what they're doing," Henry is saying. "They'll kill Captain Smith and then they'll go ahead and sail away and leave us to starve."

Channel my anger? *No!*

I can't stop myself. I run at Master Archer. I will knock him down and pummel the snot out of him.

Sixteen

Great blame and imputation was laid upon me by them for the loss of our two men which the Indians slew, insomuch that they purposed to depose me.

—Captain John Smith, *A True Relation*

IT IS EITHER Richard, or God in His mercy, who trips me. I sprawl on the ground, my face in the dirt.

"Grab him!" Master Archer orders.

"Run!" Richard cries.

But before I can scramble to my feet, Reverend Hunt lifts me by one arm and holds me fast. "He is a *boy*," he says slowly and firmly to Master Archer. "Leave him be. I will deal with him."

Master Archer wipes his bloody hand with his handkerchief. He gives me one last disgusted look, then turns to go.

Reverend Hunt drags me with him to the chapel. Richard follows.

"I'm sorry, Reverend Hunt," I say as I struggle to keep up with his long strides. He is gripping my arm so tightly it hurts. He is focusing *his* anger and most of that focus is going into my arm.

He plops me down on a log bench in the chapel. "Do not leave until you have prayed long and hard. Pray to curb your temper. Pray for humility—you will need that desperately if you become the servant of one of the gentlemen."

I hop to my feet. "I will *not* serve one of those men. They're criminals!" Then I realize what he is saying. He is assuming that at sunup, Captain Smith will be hanged and I will become another man's servant. "Are you just going to let them *kill* him?" I cry.

Reverend Hunt rubs his temples. "I have no authority here," he says quietly.

I shake my head and sink back onto the log. Richard sits next to me. I had always assumed that Reverend Hunt held the highest authority—the authority of God.

"Then can you pray for another miracle, Reverend?" Richard asks.

Reverend Hunt looks up at him, his eyes bright for a moment. He nods. "Yes," he says. "I will."

The three of us are quiet, lost in our own prayers. I pray to learn to curb my anger, but I do not ask for the humility to serve a new master.

When we leave the chapel, we find the soldiers and laborers gathered at the cook fire. They are talking in hushed tones, their eyes shifting. We draw closer and hear their plan: There are a dozen gentlemen, and over twenty of us. Yes, they have plenty of weapons, but we will have the element of surprise. Henry wants to simply slit the gentlemen's throats while they sleep, but some of the others want an all-out battle—a war.

Reverend Hunt scowls. "*No.* No killing," he says. "A war amongst ourselves will be the end of us—an end to the colony. We will not even have enough men left to fend off an Indian attack."

But the men ignore him. They want blood. And if it will save Captain Smith, so do I.

I grow weary of listening to the men argue about their plans. I nudge Richard, and we leave to walk down to the river. The afternoon sun is low. A breeze has lifted, and the river has ripples over its surface.

"Do you think their plans will work?" Richard asks me.

I shake my head. "A lot of men will die. Maybe you and I will die."

And yet, if we do nothing, we both know what will happen tomorrow morning. We will watch Captain Smith climb up the ladder to the gallows, watch them slip the noose around his neck. When they shove him off the ladder, the weight of his body will jerk his neck against the noose. Our only hope will be for his neck to break quickly so that death will come mercifully. I have seen hangings where a man gurgles and thrashes and his face turns red and death comes so slowly that I have wished for a sword to put him out of his agony.

A thin layer of ice has crusted over the water along the shoreline. I press on it with the toe of my shoe until it breaks like glass, making a star of thin lines. The wind is stiff now, and chills me right through my clothes. When I first heard about the Roanoke colony disappearing, I wondered how it could have happened so quickly. Yet here we are, down to fewer than 40 men from 105, and about to kill one another off.

I sit down heavily on the riverbank. Something on the horizon, downriver, catches my attention. I blink, then rub my eyes. It is a ship. The low winter sun has turned her sails to gold, and she is gliding toward us on the wind.

My mouth goes dry. Is this the Spanish ship we have been dreading, come to attack and kill us all? They will have an easy task. "Can you see her flag yet?" I ask slowly.

"Not yet," says Richard. His eyes are on the approaching ship as well.

A vulture circles overhead.

Then I see it, the sun catching it just right to show us the blue, white, and red. "It's an English ship!" I shout.

"Could it be Captain Newport after all this time?" Richard cries.

Reverend Hunt's words echo in my head: *I have no authority here.* But Captain Newport does have authority here, and I am sure he will not let them hang Captain Smith. I strain my neck, trying to see. Who is on board? Is there a one-armed man?

The ship glides closer. "Shouldn't we go tell them a ship is here?" Richard asks.

"Not until I see who the captain is," I say. "I want to know if Captain Smith is saved."

Then I see him, standing at the bow, looking toward shore: the one-armed captain of the ship.

Richard and I take off running up the hill to the fort. "You did it, Reverend Hunt!" I shout at the top of my lungs. "You got your miracle!"

Seventeen

The country is excellent and very rich in gold and copper. Of the gold we have brought a say [an ore sample, which proved worthless] *and hope to be with Your Lordship shortly to show it His Majesty and the rest of the lords.*

—Captain Christopher Newport,
from a letter to the Lord of Salisbury

CAPTAIN NEWPORT BRINGS so many changes it nearly makes our heads spin. Captain Smith is freed and Master Archer is taken off the council. Our cabins are suddenly crowded with sixty new colonists, and the fort becomes noisy with several new dogs, a dozen hogs, and enough chickens to coat the ground of the whole fort with their droppings. He also brings a new boy, Thomas Savage. The men tease him because of his name. "He is a savage," they say. "Send him to live with the savages."

Our storehouse is filled to overflowing with the good

things the ship has brought: wheat, pork, ale, wine, butter, and beef. We eat very well, and since this puts everyone in a good mood, there is no more talk about stealing away to England. There is a fragile peace between the gentlemen who were willing to kill us by starvation, and us commoners who were ready to murder them in their beds. It is a good thing we have the sixty new men and boys to help buffer our smoldering anger toward one another.

A few days after Captain Newport arrives we hear shouts of "*Wingapo!*" and look to see Indians paddling to shore in three canoes. "*Wingapo*, Captain Smith!" they call. When the canoes land and the Indian men begin to pull them up onshore, Richard and I go closer. The canoes are filled with bread, fish, and meat: turkey, squirrel, deer, and raccoon.

"We don't even need to trade for food," I say to Richard. "We've got so much in the storehouse now that the ship is here."

But Richard's eyes are wide, fixed on something. I follow his gaze. In one of the canoes sits a little girl. She has straight black hair, cut very short on the front and sides, and fastened in a long braid down her back. She wears several necklaces of pearls and copper, and a mantle of deerskin over one shoulder. As we watch, she jumps out of the canoe and trots up to Captain Smith. She is fairly skipping with excitement at seeing him. I hear some of what she says as she speaks to him in Algonquian, "I bring gifts from my father . . . now that you are my countryman. . . ."

The food is not for trade? It is being delivered as a *gift*?

It suddenly occurs to me who this must be. I grab Richard's arm. "It's *her*!" I whisper.

"I *know*," Richard whispers back.

We watch her as she talks to Captain Smith. She is only a child—Captain Smith says she is about ten years old—but in my mind she has become like a goddess. She is Chief Powhatan's daughter, the girl who saved Captain Smith's life, the Indian princess who has more courage than a hundred soldiers.

Suddenly, to my surprise, I hear Captain Smith say in his clumsy Algonquian, "Come meet boys. They show you my home."

My stomach does a little flip as Captain Smith leads her over to Richard and me. He tells her our names. I watch her happy, dark eyes, and keep telling myself she is only a child, no one to be so awestruck about.

"And this is Amonute," Captain Smith says to me and Richard. "But she is called 'playful one'—Pocahontas."

Pocahontas grins. "Come and show me Captain Smith's home," she says.

I translate for Richard and he nods enthusiastically. I point to our palisades. "Home—there," I say in Algonquian. It is my first time trying out my newly learned words on a native speaker, and when she understands, it feels like magic.

Pocahontas runs up the hill, nimble as a deer on her bare feet. Richard and I follow. I always thought that princesses were supposed to be quiet and proper and sit around looking royal. Not this princess.

Pocahontas peeks inside the fort gates. The men on guard look at her and raise their eyebrows. "She's the daughter of Chief Powhatan," I tell them.

Pocahontas whips her head around when she hears her father's name. Then she runs to one of our cabins to look in the door. "This is Captain Smith's house?" she asks.

"No." I shake my head. "*Peyaquaugh*," I say, and motion for her to follow me. I lead her to the cabin Captain Smith shares with Reverend Hunt, the carpenter John Laydon, and several other men.

She is fascinated with the cabin and with Captain Smith's belongings. Like a typical child, she wants to touch everything, and because she is a princess, Richard and I don't dare stop her. She sits on one of the beds and jostles it, listening to the straw crackle. She grins at herself in the shaving mirror. She looks at the muskets leaning against the wall and gives them a wide berth. I realize Captain Smith must have demonstrated his firepower to her tribe. When she sees Reverend Hunt's Bible, she opens it and gently touches the pages. I wonder if it is the first book she has ever seen. When she goes to pick up a straight razor, Richard gasps. I reach to pull it away. "Sharp," I say loudly in Algonquian. "*Bad.*"

She gives me a mischievous look, takes the blade, and runs it quickly across her arm.

Richard cries, "No!" I yelp and lunge for her. I grab the blade out of her hand. Richard grasps her arm. "Quick, get Doc Wotton!" he yells.

But Pocahontas just giggles. When we inspect her arm, there is no cut at all. She has played a trick on us!

"Can you run fast?" she asks, as if she has not just scared the living daylights out of us.

"Yes," I say. Running is something I've always been good at. "She is asking me how fast I can run," I tell Richard.

She leads us outside the cabin. She takes me by the shoulders and makes me stand facing down the main lane that goes through the center of our fort. Then she stands Richard beside me facing the same way. "We will race," she announces. It is a warm winter day, as warm as a spring day in England, and around the fort, men are outside, working on everything from repairing wattle and daub walls to shucking corn. They watch in amusement as we prepare for our race. "To the wall," she says.

I explain to Richard that we are about to race to the palisade wall. He nods in approval.

Pocahontas readies herself next to Richard. She counts with her fingers. "*Necut, ningh, nuss!*"

We run full speed down the lane, with dogs chasing and chickens squawking as they fly out of our way. I win by just a bit.

Pocahontas's face glows with sweat. "You do run fast," she says. "But I am faster. I tripped on my mantle." And with that, she pulls off her mantle. She has nothing on underneath, but she seems to not even notice that she is naked. "We will race again," she says. "I will win this time."

We line up again. I am not so ready to let a ten-year-old girl beat me. Pocahontas counts, "*Necut, ningh, nuss!*" I pump my legs as fast as they will go. But this time, freed of her mantle, Pocahontas wins easily.

"You just got beat by a girl," Richard teases.

I grumble, but Pocahontas is already on to her next idea.

"Can you do this?" she asks, and she wheels herself hand to hand and foot to foot like a cartwheel.

I try to imitate her, but I end up falling on my bum.

Pocahontas laughs, and shows us again. Richard copies her and actually does quite well. When I try again I fall on my hip and elbow, but then I start to get the hang of it. Thomas Savage sees what we are doing and comes to join us. Soon we are all able to do the cartwheels.

The men look up from their work to watch us—three English boys in dirty shirts and worn-out slops and one naked Indian princess, tumbling like cartwheels all over the fort.

CAPTAIN NEWPORT TELLS US that the soil and rocks we sent back to England were just that—dirt and rocks. There was no gold in them at all. But the Virginia Company still wants gold, and Captain Newport is convinced we can find it for them. And so, early on a frosty morning, just a week or so after the ship has arrived, a group of men gathers buckets, picks, and shovels, and sets off in search of gold to send back to England. They leave their cabins with their nighttime fires still burning. Someone from one of the cabins must have left a shirt draped over a chair near the embers, or a Bible on a table too close to the flames. Someone. Somewhere. We never did find out where the fire started.

"Fire!" someone shouts, and I look to see orange flames leap from one thatched roof to another. I snatch up a bucket and race to the river. But by the time I get back, more cabins have caught fire. Flames lick their way down the palisade, spreading like spilled wine. Men stumble through the smoke, trying to find the front gate of the fort. A soldier comes running at me, his clothes aflame. He grabs my bucket and empties the water over his head. His shirt sizzles and he gasps, slapping at the burned fabric.

I return to the river, fill my bucket again. Captain Smith is there, shouting, ordering the men into a line.

"Pass the buckets hand to hand!" he yells. We form a line that stretches from the river to the fort, and we pass the buckets quickly, one to another.

Flames leap, and thick black smoke engulfs the entire fort. One side of the palisade buckles and falls.

"Save the palisade!" someone cries. I see the men at the fort, throwing bucket after bucket onto the burning posts.

The wind blows smoke toward us and it makes me cough. Cinders and bits of ash swirl in the air. I think of nothing except passing the buckets of water, until my fingers are blistered and my arms ache.

So much work. So many weeks we spent cutting trees, splitting clapboard, tying thatch, making wattle and daub. It is all turning to ashes before our eyes.

It is afternoon before we finally quell the flames. We manage to save a good part of the palisade, but the houses are virtually gone, along with everything in them. Even Reverend Hunt's Bible is lost in the blaze. And, worst of all, the storehouse and all the food in it has been destroyed.

Eighteen

"You did promise Powhatan what was yours should be his, and he the like to you. You called him father, being in his land a stranger, and by the same reason so must I do you . . . And fear you here I should call you father? I tell you then I will, and you shall call me child, and so I will be forever and ever your countryman."

—Pocahontas speaking to Captain John Smith when they met in England in the year 1616 or 1617. Quoted by Smith in *The General History*.

WHEN I LIVED on the streets of London I was a loner. It was me against the world. But coming here to James Town has changed me. I have learned to depend on others, especially Reverend Hunt, Captain Smith, and even Richard. I have learned the importance of standing together, of cooperating. My circle has become bigger.

Now, this fire has changed all of us. Our houses, our food, even our blankets and extra clothing are gone. And it has turned cold—bone-chilling, winter cold. And yet, we have not all starved or frozen to death. Instead, our circle has become bigger.

The day after the fire, Pocahontas comes again with several men from her tribe. They have seen the smoke and are here to see if we are all right. Pocahontas runs to where Captain Smith's cabin used to be. I follow her. She stands among the ashes, bends down, and sifts through a pile of burnt wood. Then she stands and looks at me. Her eyes brim with tears.

"It is all gone," she says. "Captain Smith's house, his bed, his mirror, his beard-cutting knife . . . all gone."

I nod. She blinks, and tears run down her cheeks. She wipes them quickly away. "Captain Smith is now my brother, my countryman. My father will send gifts to help." She says it with such authority that I am reminded that she is not just a little girl, but a princess.

The Powhatan people, whom we have at times considered our enemies, now treat us as their own. They bring us deerskins and bear furs to keep us warm. Every few days they come in canoes laden with meat and bread and corn as gifts.

We start to rebuild right away, with everyone working hard. We make the fort bigger, giving it three new walls where the one wall fell down, and making it five-sided. We begin again to build houses.

January stretches into February and it turns even colder. The night air sucks the warmth from our bones as we try to sleep in tents made from the ship's sails. Without the skins and furs from the Powhatans, we would all freeze. As it is, we sometimes awake in the morning to find one of our men—the oldest, weakest, and sickest among us—frozen in his bed. And once again, digging graves is part of my regular chores.

We make a very interesting trade. We send Thomas Savage to Werowocomoco to live, and Chief Powhatan sends us his servant boy, Namontack, to live with us. Our circles widen even more, and I think it is a good way to live. We are standing on many legs now, together with the Powhatans. I think of the centipedes that used to crawl over my bed last summer, and think we are like them, with so many legs. A centipede does not topple in a storm.

Namontack, our new tent mate, is fourteen years old, or fourteen returns of the leaf as he puts it. Because he is a servant, he wears no copper or pearls. In fact, he wears no mantle even in the cold weather, only leggings and breechcloth. Namontack has bright eyes and a quick smile. He is taller than I am, and strong-looking, too. I certainly wouldn't want to race him—I'm sure he would beat me by a mile.

Reverend Hunt says it is very good that Namontack has come to live with us. The reverend has been impatient to win the souls of the natives for Christ. "We will teach the boy English," Reverend Hunts says, "and then I will tell him the good news of Christ, and he will bring that message to his people." And so Reverend Hunt spends each morning teaching Namontack a few English words.

Namontack teaches me more Algonquian words as we work alongside each other with the house building, and I am getting much better at the language. One day we are splitting clapboard, and he shakes his head. "Our houses are better," he says in Algonquian. He has been telling me almost daily what things are better at his home, and so I am not surprised. "We do not take big trees down to build our houses." He goes on to tell me how their houses are built with frames made of thin saplings. The walls and roofs are made of mats woven from rushes. He says they are much warmer than our drafty houses. I try to imagine his village, Werowocomoco, and hope that soon I will be allowed on one of Captain Smith's exploration trips so that I'll see an Indian village for myself.

Namontack shakes his head again and frowns. "Our tribe is better than your tribe," he says. "Your tribe has no women. I do not understand why Chief Powhatan brought you into the Powhatan empire. A tribe with no women and children is not worth much."

My jaw drops. "Us in Powhatan empire?" I ask in my halting Algonquian.

"Yes," Namontack says with the patience one uses when explaining something to a small child. "Captain Smith was adopted into our tribe. He became a son to Chief

Powhatan. Captain Smith is your ruler, your *werowance*, and so now your tribe belongs to Chief Powhatan. You are Powhatan people. What happens to one of us happens to all of us—that is why we took care of you after the fire."

"Captain Smith *adopted*?" I squeak.

Namontack nods. "He died as an Englishman, and came back to life as a Powhatan man."

I picture Captain Smith, his head held down on a rock, with men ready to bash his brains out—*or were they*?

"Pocahontas make Captain Smith no death?" I struggle to find the words to ask my question.

"Yes. Yes," Namontack says, grinning.

I am relieved. So they really did almost kill Captain Smith.

But then Namontack adds, "Pocahontas was perfect at the ceremony. Chief Powhatan chose her to save Captain Smith because she is his favorite among all of his daughters."

I bury my face in my hands. It was *theater*. A ritual. They were acting out death and rebirth, and Pocahontas was part of an act.

Namontack asks me what is wrong, why am I holding my head in my hands. I tell him I am just tired.

Now it all makes sense: the gifts of food and animal furs, the sudden peace between us. Chief Powhatan is taking care of us because he considers us one of his tribes. If it were just me, I would be very happy with the arrangement. It means survival and peace. It means an end to the bloodshed between our settlers and the Powhatans. But I know these gentlemen, and I know they have no interest in being the subjects of a man they consider to be a lowly savage. I also know that President Ratcliffe would be quite surprised to find out that Chief Powhatan thinks Captain Smith is our real ruler. My hope is that, with no one to explain it to them, the gentlemen simply won't find out that Powhatan now considers us his subjects.

BY SPRING WE HAVE dug a well for clean, fresh water. We have also built enough houses for everyone, and a new church for Reverend Hunt to hold our daily services in. Captain Newport's ship is again loaded with rocks that we hope contain gold. I have not totally given up on my dream of riches from this New World, but those hopes have certainly dimmed.

The ship also carries three new passengers: Master Wingfield and Master Archer are being sent back to England in dishonor. And Namontack is going to England so that he can come back and tell Chief Powhatan all about it.

Namontack shows me a stick Chief Powhatan has given him. "I will count the people and make marks on the stick," he says. "I will be able to tell Chief Powhatan how many people there are in your land."

I laugh, remembering the teeming streets of London, with carriages and horses and people and hogs all vying for space on the cobblestones. I think of Namontack walking along the docks—the same docks I left so many months ago—and seeing our world for the first time. I wonder what he will think of St. Paul's Church, with its pinnacles and tower rising high as Virginia trees, or the rows and rows of wattle and daub houses with gangs of dirty children playing out front. How the English will stare at him with his deerskin breechcloth and bare chest! I think he will need many, many sticks to count all the people in England, but I don't tell him so. I say good-bye and wish him a safe voyage.

The summer of 1608 is much better than the summer of 1607. We now have fresh water from our well, houses for everyone instead of tents, and peace with the natives. Captain Smith continues our trading, so food is plentiful. Still, a sickness comes upon us—we now call it the "summer sickness"—and many of our men are too weak to work.

There are the usual conjectures about what it can be, the usual suspicion that there is a Spanish spy among us who is slipping ratsbane into our food and drink. But Reverend Hunt says he thinks it has something to do with the mosquitoes. We get sick as soon as they start to buzz and bite.

One day, while Captain Smith is away on an exploration trip up the river, President Ratcliffe makes a decision that costs him his presidency. He decides he wants a large house in the woods—a house befitting a president—and that the lot of us hot, itchy, feverish men and boys will build it for him. He forces us to work with the threat of whipping if we refuse. By the time Captain Smith returns a week later and finds out what is going on, we are angry as a nest of hornets.

"He's worse than Wingfield!" Henry shouts.

"He's been eating more than his share of the stores and lying idle while we sweat and faint in the heat," Nathaniel complains.

"He's unfit to be president!" John Laydon declares.

There is more angry discussion, and by the end of the day it is decided: Captain Ratcliffe will no longer be our president. He will be sent back to England with the next supply ship.

Then, the debate begins about who should be our new president. It must be a man who cares about the whole colony, not just himself and a few friends. They want someone who is fair and willing to do his share of the work, not sit idle giving orders. They want someone who has been here since the beginning, who knows about how to survive in Virginia. When they make their choice, I am amazed and proud.

Captain John Smith will be our new president.

Nineteen

"You must obey this now for a law that he that will not work shall not eat, *except by sickness he be disabled. For the labors of thirty or forty honest and industrious men shall not be consumed to maintain an hundred and fifty idle loiterers."*

—Captain John Smith, quoted in
William Symonds, ed., *The Proceedings*

ON SEPTEMBER 10, 1608, Captain John Smith takes the oath of office and becomes our new president. He officially decrees: "He that will not work shall not eat," and he holds us to it. Gentleman or not, any man who wants supper has to pitch in.

But even with this decree, he is well liked. Unlike Presidents Wingfield and Ratcliffe before him, Captain Smith divides the rations equally with us and works right alongside us sharing the burdens, too. And he stays in the cabin he has always shared with Reverend Hunt, John

Laydon, and others. There will be no mansion in the woods for President Smith. There are a few gentlemen left from the group who tried to run off on the *Discovery* with our food, and I sometimes hear grumbling from them, but they are far outnumbered now by men—new settlers and old—who have great respect and trust for Captain Smith.

So now I am the page of a ruler. It is the most important I have ever felt in my life. I wish my mum could know, and I hope she does know, taking a peek down from heaven now and then. She would also be very surprised to see that a commoner is our president. I think it would make her happy to know that here in the New World, the gentlemen don't hold all of the power.

Captain Smith continues to write our story. He is also drawing maps of the rivers and land he has found on his exploration trips. I am relieved to find out that not all of his writings were destroyed in the fire—some of the pages had already been sent back to England with Captain Newport.

One day in late September, Richard and I are in the field harvesting vegetables. We have grown them the way Namontack taught us, planting the corn and beans together in a mound, so that the bean plants can climb the cornstalks. Suddenly we hear shouts from the river front. "Ship ashore!" and a few moments later, "She flies the British flag!"

Richard and I stop working and look at each other. "Could it be Captain Newport so soon?" Richard asks.

I look at the baskets of beans and squash we've already gathered. I hope we've done enough work to earn our supper and that no one will mind if we go to greet the ship. "Let's go see," I say.

Other men come to the riverfront as well. We watch as the ship glides toward shore. Captain Newport is at her helm.

"Another crowd of colonists to feed, no doubt," Henry grumbles.

"Let's hope they've sent us more skilled workers and fewer gentlemen, as I requested," says President Smith.

The ship anchors, the longboat is lowered, and the first few passengers began to climb down the rope ladder. The late afternoon sun glints in my eyes, and at first I think that what I am seeing is a trick of the light. But then I hear the men around me, as amazed as I am.

"Could it be?"

"My Lord, it's a vision!"

"How could they send *women* to this godforsaken place?"

As the longboat nears us, men trip over one another rushing to help. "Let me give her a hand!" "No, let *me* give her a hand!"

I'm surprised we don't have a fistfight before the longboat even lands. In the boat are a number of men, but all any of us see are the two women, sitting straight-backed, clutching satchels.

One of the women is older, and large, with a round face and double chin. The other woman—a girl, really—has pale skin and dark, frightened eyes. A few black curls peek out from under her coif.

I listen to the conversation as the longboat passengers are introduced to President Smith: Master Francis West, Master Daniel Tucker, Master and Mrs. Thomas Forrest, and Mrs. Forrest's servant girl, Ann Burras.

It has been a very long time since we have seen English women. It gives me a twinge of sadness, of missing my mother, to see their colorful petticoats—indigo blue and saffron yellow—and white coifs. It feels familiar, like home.

Miss Ann Burras squints her eyes, scowls, and ignores the men who are jostling one another to have a chance to carry her satchel. She holds tight to that satchel and turns her back to them. I feel sorry for her, being the center of attention like that when she obviously doesn't want to be.

Namontack is on the next longboat trip to shore. I am surprised to see that he is wearing a linen shirt. But England did not change him too much—his hair is still shaved close on one side and long on the other, and his eyes are still bright. He beams at me. "Hello, Samuel, how are you?" he calls out in accented English. "I am now a world traveler!"

I laugh. "You are speaking English well, my friend!" I call to him. I realize that in his months away, with no one to speak Algonquian with, he has had plenty of time to learn the English language—much more than the few words and phrases Reverend Hunt taught him before he left. "Namontack, where is your stick?" I ask. "Did you make lots of notches in it?"

Namontack shakes his head. "Too many people," he says. "I throw stick in river."

Reverend Hunt is very happy that Namontack is now speaking English so well. He wastes no time, but sits him down to tell him about God the Father, Jesus the Son, and the Holy Spirit, and how he must bring the message of salvation to the other Powhatans.

Namontack nods enthusiastically. "Yes, yes. I learn of your gods in England. And I tell them of my gods." He launches into a lively description of Okeus, the vengeful god, who requires sacrifices of tobacco, copper, beads, and sometimes animal blood, and sends punishment if he is not made happy. He tells us about Ahone, the god who is all-loving, all-forgiving, who makes the sun shine and ripens the crops. And he tells us of the great respect his people have for the spirit of life that is in all things—people, animals, plants, fire, water, wind. . . .

Reverend Hunt shakes his head. "There is only one God, maker of heaven and earth." Reverend Hunt tells us the story of creation, how God made the world and all things in it in six days, and rested on the seventh day, the Sabbath.

Again, Namontack nods with interest. "Now I tell you how *our* world was made," he says. He tells us a story about the Great Hare who created different kinds of men and women and put them in a big sack. He protected them from giants who wanted to eat them. The Great Hare filled the rivers with fish and put deer upon the land. Then he took the men and women out of the sack and put them in different places on the earth to live.

I enjoy Namontack's story, but I can see that Reverend Hunt is becoming discouraged. Namontack does not understand that he is to give up his gods and his stories and take the word of God from the Bible back to his people. Reverend Hunt begins to explain again, but Captain Smith finds us boys sitting idle and tells Reverend Hunt he needs us to come work in the gardens. I put on my straw hat and pick up a basket. I hope Reverend Hunt is not too disappointed that his first time trying to convert a Virginia native to Christianity did not work out.

CAPTAIN NEWPORT HAS brought us seventy new colonists, stores, and the news that the rocks we sent to England were, once again, just rocks. The Virginia Company has a new idea about how we can make a profit: We are to use the raw materials we have here in Virginia and begin making glass, pitch, tar, and soap-ashes to send back to England. They've sent us several Polish and German tradesmen to get us started with these projects. They have already begun to build a glasshouse a little way from our fort, with a large furnace for glass-making.

Captain Newport has also brought orders from the Virginia Company to place an English crown on Chief Powhatan's head, making him a prince under King James and making all of his people English subjects. My mind reels when I hear this. Chief Powhatan thinks *we* are *his* subjects, and now they want to make *Powhatan's* people *English* subjects? The whole thing tangles my brain in knots.

If the thought of being Chief Powhatan's subjects would be distasteful to the gentlemen, then I imagine that becoming subjects of King James would be just as distasteful to the Powhatan people. Especially after they hear Namontack's report on King James, whom he met while he was in London.

"Our Chief Powhatan is much better than your king," Namontack says, speaking in Algonquian so that the gentlemen will not hear his assessment of our exalted king. "Your king is a short, weak man. Our chief is tall and very strong. Your king has no hair and no teeth, just a round belly from eating too much. How can such a man be king?" A look of disgust crosses Namontack's face, as if he is not quite sure how to tell me his next point. "And he . . . stinks. Does he not bathe? And he drinks wine until he can no longer speak or stand."

I have heard these stories about our King James. It is well known that the king's doctors have warned him that bathing causes the plague, and he has taken this advice to heart. He almost never bathes. Yet Englishmen still honor him. He is, after all, our king. Namontack feels no such obligation. The natives bathe quite often, even in cold weather. They have no fear of the English plague, only disdain for English stink.

"Our Chief Powhatan is a true king," says Namontack. "He is powerful and honorable."

I am about to have my first chance to meet the great Chief Powhatan. Captain Smith is taking me and Namontack, along with three other men, over land to Werowocomoco. We will bring an invitation to Chief Powhatan to come to James Town to receive gifts from King James and to be crowned. Captain Smith is angry at the whole plan—very angry.

"Make an emperor into a prince? Ask an emperor to travel to receive gifts? I assure you, this will not sit well with Chief Powhatan," he says. "He is king here in his own country. What right does King James have, from across an ocean, to make him his subject? Power is like weights in a balance. No one gains power without someone else losing power, and Chief Powhatan does not want to lose any of his power. It has been a long, hard road to peace with Chief Powhatan, but if he understands what this coronation means, it may well be the end of our peace."

Captain Newport refuses to budge. He is bound to carry out the orders from the Virginia Company. And so Captain Smith prepares for our journey to Werowocomoco.

In the meantime, Miss Ann Burras is making quite an impression at James Town. She is almost always busy taking care of Mrs. Forrest, a very plump gentlewoman who hasn't figured out yet that life in James Town will be a lot harder than life in England. She is constantly making demands on Ann: Heat some water, wash these clothes, get supper on the table. Mrs. Forrest insists on having her meals in her cabin with her husband instead of eating from the communal cook pot with the rest of us.

During the rare moments Ann is not busy, she has every unmarried man in the colony trying to get her attention. Even Nathaniel, who is sixteen by now, makes a fool of himself, strutting around in his armor, making a show of his musket and sword. There are at least two or three fistfights a day, and I've no doubt they are because of Miss Ann Burras. She is fourteen years old, so she is of marriageable age, and I suspect we will have a wedding before too long.

One day, Richard, Namontack, and I are sent to repair the fishnets and bring back the catch for supper. We are the only ones at the riverfront when Ann comes down to fill buckets with water.

"Here, we can fill them," Richard offers. "We're already barefoot and wet." He takes the buckets from her.

Ann doesn't smile or say thank you, she just looks away. It is as if she has become afraid to look anyone in the eye for fear they will try to court her. *We're just boys,* I want to say. *We'll be your friends.*

While we fill the buckets, Ann walks to where some wildflowers are growing and picks a small bouquet of yellow, purple, and white. Then, it seems as if my unspoken message has somehow gotten through, because she comes and sits down near us. "A moment of peace," she says, and rubs her sore shoulders.

"Your mistress works you hard," I say. I do not add what I have been thinking for weeks: *You'll never live through the winter if you stay so skinny and tired.* And I don't ask what I have been suspicious about: *Is your mistress eating some of your food rations?*

Ann shrugs. "No harder than I worked in England," she says. But I know this cannot be true.

"President Smith says if we don't work we don't get to eat," says Richard. "I don't see your mistress doing much work, but by the looks of her, she does a whole lot of eating!"

Richard, Namontack, and I laugh, but Ann scowls. "Don't insult my mistress," she scolds. But we can't help ourselves, and soon she breaks down and laughs with us.

When we settle, Ann says, "Mistress Forrest makes me work every moment because she is afraid I'll find a beau." She blushes as she says it. "Her husband says I should marry, but she wants to keep me as her maid."

"You have found this beau?" Namontack asks.

Ann shakes her head.

"She's found about a hundred of them!" Richard exclaims, and this starts us all laughing again.

Finally Ann sighs. "I'd better get back or I'll get a beating for dawdling," she says.

We help her balance the yoke across her shoulders and lift the buckets of water. As I watch her walk back to the fort, I think that Mrs. Forrest should be made to do her own chores, and that Ann's best chance of making it through the winter will be to get away from that demanding woman.

When she is gone, Richard asks, "Who do you think she'll marry if she gets permission?"

"Maybe your *werowance*, Captain Smith?" Namontack suggests.

I shake my head. "He's the only unmarried man *not* courting her. He must be too busy for marriage."

As we repair the fishnets we have fun guessing who Miss Ann Burras will pick if she gets permission to wed. I only hope she finds someone who will be kind to her and make sure she gets her full food rations. I have never dug a grave for a girl before, and I don't want to start now.

Twenty

Thus did they show their feats of arms,
and others art in dancing.
Some other us'd their oaten pipe,
and others voices chanting.

—William Symonds, ed., *The Proceedings*

THE MORNING WE are to leave for Werowocomoco I am jittery with excitement. Namontack is, too—it will be his first time home since he went to England. He will have lots of stories to tell his people. "You will love my home," he says to me. "It is—"

"I know," I interrupt him. "It is much better than my home."

We both laugh.

Namontack collects the gifts he received in England: a red velvet cassock, which he says is not as warm as a deerskin mantle; a pewter chalice, which he says is not as good as a gourd to drink out of; and an ivory tooth scraper, which he refuses to use because he says the Indian way of cleaning his teeth, with a sassafras root, is much better.

I gather my spoon and bowl and a waterskin. We present ourselves to Captain Smith, each with a small bundle to carry. Captain Smith looks up from cleaning his musket. "Samuel, where is your sword? Where is your armor? Go back and get properly attired."

But I thought we were at peace with the Powhatans, I want to say. I know better than to argue with Captain Smith so I simply go to my cabin and do as he says. At least he is not making me carry my heavy musket on the hike to Werowocomoco.

When I get back to Captain Smith's cabin, the carpenter John Laydon is sitting out front with his tools, working at making a small wooden chest. He is carving initials into the top of the chest. He already has an *A* and as I watch, he finishes a *B*.

"Who is that for?" I ask.

He keeps his eyes cast down, intent on his work, and does not answer me.

Then it dawns on me. I tip my head close to his. "Is it for *her*?" I whisper.

He glances at me and I see he is afraid to tell me, afraid I will announce it and give the other men a chance to ridicule him.

I look at the small chest. It is beautifully crafted out

of cherrywood. A work of love. I watch him as he begins to carve a border around the initials. John Laydon is a quiet man. He is sturdy and kind. And he is the only man who has decided to woo Miss Ann Burras with something other than bragging and strutting. I lean close again. "She likes flowers, too," I say.

He gives me a quick smile and continues his work.

Captain Smith is ready to go. He carries his musket and has not one, but two bandoleers of gunpowder strung across his chest. His sword hangs at his side, and he is wearing full armor. He looks like he is going into battle, not like he is visiting someone to invite them to come get some presents. This crowning of Powhatan must truly be a bad idea.

THERE ARE ONLY six of us going: me, Captain Smith, Namontack, and three soldiers. We hike over land for about twelve miles. When we come to the Pamunkey River, which separates us from Werowocomoco, we find a canoe in the rushes and use it to paddle across.

When we reach the other side I see nothing but the tall, grand trees with their leaves turning red and gold. "Come," says Namontack. "*Peyaquaugh.*"

A worn footpath brings us into the woods, and soon I smell the smoke from cook fires. Namontack breathes deeply and smiles. He is coming home.

We come to where the houses of Werowocomoco are gathered—straw-colored rectangular houses with curved roofs. There are at least twenty of them scattered among the trees, with gardens in between. They are about the size of ours, but made of rushes woven together. Three small boys run out to greet us. Namontack lifts the littlest one into the air. He laughs and says, in Algonquian, "You grew so much while I was gone. You must have eaten a whole bear!"

More people from the village come to see who has arrived. Captain Smith speaks with one of the elders. He tells him we have gifts for Chief Powhatan, brought from England. Will the great chief come to James Town to receive his gifts? The elder says that Chief Powhatan is in another village, thirty miles away. He will send for him immediately, but he will not arrive until tomorrow. I am relieved. We do not have to anger Chief Powhatan quite yet.

It is beginning to get dark, and the air is filled with the chirping of crickets and cicadas. The elder motions for us to follow him, and he leads us to a field. Two young boys lay down mats for us to sit on, and then they build a fire. Are we being invited for supper? Are they about to start cooking on the fire, I wonder?

We sit on the mats and various people from the village come to sit near us—a few old men and women, many children and young warriors. They are all silent, their faces expectant, as if they are waiting for something to happen. But no one brings food to cook on the fire. My stomach begins to churn. What is going on? What are they expecting to happen? I am glad I have my sword, but *what are they going to do to us*?

Captain Smith sits on the mat next to me. His eyes are wary, and I know that he, too, suspects this might be a trap. I touch his sleeve. "What are they *doing*?" I whisper.

Suddenly, shrieking and howling erupt from the forest—the same battle cries I heard the night James was killed! I leap to my feet and pull out my sword, ready to fight and slash.

Captain Smith draws his sword. He seizes an old man sitting near us, and holds the sword to his throat. Our soldiers aim their muskets into the dark forest. The howling comes closer, louder. Our attackers will be upon us any moment.

Out of the shadows a little girl comes running. She rushes up to us and stands bravely in front of the loaded muskets. It is Pocahontas.

"I promise, no harm will come to you," she says, holding out her hands, palms up. "If I am wrong, you may kill me."

Captain Smith lets go of the old man. He translates what Pocahontas has said for the soldiers, and they slowly lower their muskets. "All right," Captain Smith says, still looking wary.

Pocahontas recognizes me and smiles. She comes to me and Captain Smith and gives us that same look of expectancy I've been seeing all evening. "Just *watch*," she says. Then, in English she adds, "You like."

I grin. Captain Smith must have taught her some English words during her visits to our fort and his visits to her village. She takes our hands, pulls us both down onto our mats, and settles in between us.

The fire casts a moving light. Into that firelight leaps a form. Is it a buck? I blink. It is a *woman*. She is wearing the horns of a buck. Another woman leaps into the light, then another, and another, all dancing, shrieking their battle cries, their bodies painted white and black and red. Some wear bucks' horns on their heads and each carries a weapon—one a club, another a sword, another a bow and arrows. The young women leap and whirl around the fire, their battle cries now mixing with the music of drums and rattles. They bring the night alive with their warrior's dance.

I watch, spellbound. It is magic. The music and dancing lasts for at least an hour. Then the women run off into the darkness of the forest, shrieking the same as when they came. There is a moment of hushed silence. Then everyone starts talking, laughing, with children running and playing, and everyone getting up from their mats.

Pocahontas looks at me, her eyes glowing. "Did you like it?" she asks in Algonquian.

I nod enthusiastically. "*Wow!*" I say. This is a new Algonquian word I learned from Namontack. *Wow* is their word for wonder and awe, and it is definitely the best word to describe what I have seen. I have heard about the masquerades in England, with their grand costumes and music and acting, but only nobles are allowed to see them. Now I have seen a New World masquerade while sitting next to a princess!

With torches lighting our way, Pocahontas leads us back into the village to one of the houses. There, the young women dancers join us, still in their costumes of body paint. They all act as if they are in love with Captain Smith and our soldiers. They crowd around them giggling and saying, in English, "Love you not me? Love you not me?"

I raise my eyebrows at Pocahontas. "Who teach them *that*?" I ask.

She gives me an impish look and shrugs.

I smell something delicious and turn to see several older women bringing in platters of food. There are large wooden bowls of steaming beans, peas and squash, platters of roasted fish and venison, baskets of bread and fruit. It is a *feast*.

I eat until I can't stuff in another bite. When Namontack sees me yawning, he takes me by the shoulders and steers me toward the door. "You will sleep in my house tonight," he says.

Outside the night air is brisk, but when we enter Namontack's house it is toasty warm from a fire in the middle of the dirt floor. The smoke gathers in the high ceiling and escapes through a hole in the roof. Lining the walls, there are platforms made with poles, reed mats, and skins. I see that Namontack's brothers, the three little boys who greeted him when we arrived, are already asleep on the platforms. He points to where I will sleep, next to the smallest boy. He gives me a deerskin blanket to keep me warm.

As I lie on the bed I can still hear the talking and laughing coming from the house where the feast is going on. *Namontack is right*, I think. *His home is much better than James Town.* There is more food and more joy to be had in one night here than in a whole year in James Town. Thomas Savage only stayed for a little while in Werowocomoco; why did he not beg to be allowed to stay forever? I wish I could come here to live. I would learn the Algonquian language even better, and I would be able to trade and help the colony. Namontack could teach me to make a bow and arrows and to shoot straight. I could hunt, and help to feed us. I wonder if this is what Reverend Hunt means about making decisions out of love—love for our newfound Indian friends, love for our fragile New World colony.

I remember when we first landed in Virginia, and again the night of the Indian raid, how I thought I hated all of the natives and I wanted our men to shoot them and kill them. Those thoughts seem so strange to me now, now that Namontack has become my friend and Chief Powhatan has rescued us from cold and starvation, and the princess Pocahontas has treated us as her countrymen. This New World is a good place to live, I think, as long as we live in peace with the Powhatan people.

Then I remember how Captain Smith dressed as a warrior to bring news of the coronation to Chief Powhatan, how he said this news would not sit well with the chief. And I wonder how long the peace, and the love, will last.

Twenty-One

> *"If your king have sent me presents, I also am a king and this is my land. Eight days I will stay to receive them. Your father* [Captain Newport] *is to come to me, not I to him nor yet to your fort, neither will I bite at such a bait."*
>
> —Chief Powhatan, quoted in William Symonds, ed., *The Proceedings*

IT IS MORNING when I see Wahunsonacock, the Great Powhatan, for the first time. He is tall and imposing, strong and regal. He wears a necklace of a large piece of copper, and many strings of beads. If copper and beads are the Powhatan gold and jewels, then he must truly be wealthy.

Captain Smith delivers his message: Will the great chief come to James Town to receive his gifts from King James? I see immediately that Captain Smith was right—an emperor should not be invited to come to another town to receive gifts. Chief Powhatan's eyes flash with anger.

"Your king has sent me presents?" he demands. "I also am a king and this is my land." He splays his arms and fingers to show this is *all* his land. "I will wait here eight days to receive the gifts. Captain Newport is to come to *me*, not I to him."

On the hike back to James Town, Captain Smith stomps his anger into the woodland path. "They know *nothing*," he shouts. "Those Virginia Company investors sit in their velvet chairs and dream up what they want to accomplish here. They know nothing of the reality of what is here, and they're going to get us killed. They are idiots!"

I keep my eyes on the ground, and the soldiers do the same. None of us wants to say a word to Captain Smith when he is this angry.

"Who ever heard of making an emperor into a prince?" he continues. "Yet that is what they are trying to do." He kicks a fallen branch out of his way. "No good will come of this. Mark my words—no good *at all*."

Back in James Town, Captain Smith delivers Chief Powhatan's message. Captain Newport frowns, but he is still determined to obey the orders from the Virginia Company: Chief Powhatan must be crowned a prince under King James. Captain Newport says he will travel to Werowocomoco to accomplish this task.

Though the trip is only twelve miles across land, it

is much longer by boat. Powhatan's gifts—an English bed, furniture, a copper pot, a wash basin and pitcher, a red cloak, shoes, and that troublesome crown—are loaded onto a barge for the hundred-mile trip down the James River (or the Powhatan River, depending on who you are talking to), into the Chesapeake Bay and up the Pamunkey River to Werowocomoco.

Captain Newport and his men return from the coronation a week later.

Captain Smith does not even ask them how it all went. He is still fuming.

The soldiers who were there tell us the story. Chief Powhatan was asked to kneel to receive his crown. He pretended to not understand. Captain Newport demonstrated the kneeling over and over again until he looked like a marionette on strings and people began to snicker. Still Chief Powhatan acted as if he did not understand. He absolutely would not kneel. Captain Smith nods smugly when he hears this. "He understood perfectly," he says. "And he refused to lower himself."

Finally, Captain Newport ordered two soldiers to push down hard on Chief Powhatan's shoulders. This made the chief take one quick tripping step, and in that moment they placed the crown on his head. Then they shot off a round of musket fire to celebrate. Chief Powhatan was now officially a subject of King James I of England.

"He is happy with his new position," Captain Newport says. "He gave me his mantle as a gift in return."

But another soldier fills us in on the rest. "He gave the mantle—and it is a beauty—because he really liked the bed and wash basin, copper pot, and whatnot. But do you know what else he gave Captain Newport? A pair of worn-out, sweaty, smelly old moccasins. I'll bet he spit in them, too. *That's* what he thinks of that crown. Let me tell you, Chief Powhatan is a proud emperor. He does not want to be a prince under our King James."

Especially not after he has heard from Namontack that King James is a short, flabby, weak man with no teeth and the strongest body odor in London.

I have a bad feeling in the pit of my stomach. It has all been a big mistake—a mistake we cannot undo. "What will happen now?" I ask Captain Smith.

"Trouble," he says, his anger smoldering. "Trouble that *we* will have to bear, while the fools who gave these orders sit in their comfortable homes in London, and while Captain Newport sails safely back to England."

THE FIRST THING we get is not trouble, but a wedding. Ann has permission to marry, and she has said yes to John Laydon. I am convinced she made a good choice. One night when it rained so hard all of our cabins were flooding, John Laydon was outside Master and Mistress

Forrest's cabin, where Ann lives, digging a trench instead of trying to save his own cabin from the flood. I believe he will be a good husband to her.

We gather in the chapel, Ann in her burgundy Sunday petticoat and yellow bodice, and John in his just-washed shirt with a blue doublet. Reverend Hunt performs the service, and we have a good meal afterward, with several chickens sacrificed for the celebration. The trees surround us with their fall leaves in blazes of red and orange and yellow, as if they, too, are celebrating the first English wedding in the New World.

Reverend Hunt is in good spirits for the wedding, but he has been feeling poorly off and on for months now. It is as if the summer sickness never left him. He has headaches and fevers that sometimes send him to his bed.

A few days after the wedding, Reverend Hunt takes to his bed again. Richard takes good care of him, but I also check on him often to see if he needs water or food or other comfort. I wonder if there is something, some food or herb or medicine, that I can bring him that will heal him this time the way the eggs and meat and wine healed him before.

One day when I check on him, he asks me for some water. His hands shake as he takes the goblet from me. He drinks, then looks me in the eye.

"Samuel, you will not always be a servant," he says. "You will do something far greater than that."

I am surprised by this sudden announcement. I shake my head. I am an orphan, the son of dead peasants. Of course I will always be a servant—what else could I be, I wonder?

"You must learn from what you see around you," he says. "Learn from Captain Smith—President Smith. Do you know why he is well liked as president while President Wingfield and President Ratcliffe were not?"

I know the answer because I have already thought about it. "It is because Captain Smith cares about all of us," I say. "The other leaders cared only for their own comfort and their own gain, and for the gain of a few of their friends."

Reverend Hunt nods. "Good. You are already learning. This is important for you to remember because I will not always be here to remind you." He lies back down and closes his eyes.

"But . . . if I will not always be a servant, what *will* I be?" I ask. Could I become a soldier? Even an officer like Captain Smith?

Reverend Hunt smiles with his eyes closed. "You will see," he says. "Remember what we have talked about here. And remember that you will always know the right decision because it is when you choose from love."

He looks as if he has talked enough. I take a rag, wring it out in a bowl of cool water, and lay it on his forehead. He is so pale and seems so weak—it is the worst I have seen him. My chest feels heavy with sadness. Reverend Hunt was the first person I opened my heart to after it was closed up tight when my mum died. I can't stand to see life slipping away from him like this. I wonder if I might lay my hands on his head and pray, and keep his soul from leaving his body the way he did for me many months ago. But, I realize, if God is ready to take Reverend Hunt up to heaven, it is not my business to try to stop Him.

"Would you like some supper?" I ask Reverend Hunt quietly.

He shakes his head slightly.

I touch his hand and leave him to rest.

Reverend Hunt does not leave his bed again. Richard and I keep a vigil, one or the other of us checking on him each hour. Finally, he stops asking for food or water and wants only to lie still. I know it is my last chance to speak to him. I go in the evening, light a candle, and kneel by his bed.

"Reverend Hunt," I whisper.

He opens his eyes for a moment and nods, and I know he is listening.

What do I want to say? *Don't leave. Please stay. Pray for another miracle!* I shake my head to stop these thoughts. *He is leaving*, I tell myself firmly. *You can't stop it.*

"Reverend Hunt, thank you for teaching me," I say. I force myself to talk past the lump in my throat. "Thank you for treating me like I was worth something."

The day we bury Reverend Hunt it is rainy and cold. My feet sink into the mud at the grave site. Richard stands with me, both of us silent. They shoot off the cannons in Reverend Hunt's honor; a great man has gone to his reward in heaven.

Twenty-Two

"Captain Smith, you shall find Powhatan to use you kindly, but trust him not; . . . for he hath sent for you only to cut your throats."

—Chief of the Warraskoyacks, quoted in William Symonds, ed., *The Proceedings*

OUR TROUBLE STARTS when winter sets in. If we had more skilled farmers and hunters, and if we all worked at farming and hunting, we might be able to produce enough food to get us through the winter. But as it is, our men are kept busy searching for gold, digging sassafras, and making clapboard, glass, pitch, tar, and soap-ashes to ship back to England, in the hopes that something in the lot will make a profit for the Virginia Company. And to make things worse, when Captain Newport leaves in December, he takes a lot of our food stores with him, saying he and his sailors will need them for the long voyage home. At least he takes Captain Ratcliffe as well, and rids us of him.

When our barrels are close to empty, Captain Smith goes to trade with the natives for grain. But he comes back empty-handed. Chief Powhatan has commanded all of his tribes not to trade with us.

"He is wielding his power," says Captain Smith. "He is showing us that the crowning ceremony angered him, and that his power is not diminished by it. We will see what else he plans to do."

We are allowed one cup of grain for each person each day. I am always hungry. I often think of the feast at Werowocomoco and wish I was there again. Richard and I dig up sassafras root to chew on to ease our hunger. Then we talk about food, trying to use our minds to fill our bellies.

"My mum used to make Yorkshire pudding at Christmastime," I say. "With the crust just a little brown, and loads of gravy."

Richard closes his eyes, imagining. "And remember All Saints' Day at the orphanage?" he asks. "When we had stew with enough meat in it so everyone got some?"

We talk about the birds and fish we roasted on Nevis, and I tell him again about the mounds of peas, squash, and venison at the Werowocomoco feast. Soon our jaws are tired from chewing on the sassafras roots, and for a time our bellies are fooled into thinking we have eaten.

Then, one day we have good news—or what seems like good news. Two natives arrive to tell us that Chief Powhatan is ready to trade. He will give us food if we bring him what he wants: a grindstone, a rooster and a hen, copper, beads, fifty swords, several muskets, and workmen to build him an English-style house. He knows we are hungry enough that Captain Smith might well give him all he wants, including the weapons.

President Smith rubs his forehead and says quietly, "We are desperate for the food." To the messengers, in Algonquian, he says, "Tell Chief Powhatan we come, give things he wants."

But as the messengers walk away, he says in English, "Except the guns and swords. I will throw in some extra gifts instead."

I smile. Watching the battle of wills between Captain Smith and Chief Powhatan is like watching the dance of a sword fight between two proud, powerful men.

WE LOAD UP two barges and the *Discovery* for the trip to Werowocomoco. We hope to bring all three of the vessels back laden with food.

The first night we stop at the Warraskoyack village and are welcomed as guests. Chief Sasenticum shares his pipe of tobacco with Captain Smith, and shares some advice as well. I listen hard to understand the Algonquian words. "Chief Powhatan will treat you kindly, but do not trust him," he says. "He has sent for you only to slit your throats."

Captain Smith does not seem surprised, and I realize he has already guessed that this might be a trap. "We keep guns ready," he says in his choppy Algonquian. Then he looks at me. "I leave boy with you?" he asks Chief Sasenticum. "I send messenger to him. If I dead, boy go to James Town, tell others."

This chills me to my bones. I want to object, to tell Captain Smith not to go. Why is he willingly walking into a trap? We are surviving on our grain, I want to tell him. Captain Newport will be back soon. Let us all return to James Town tomorrow and wait for the supply ship. But I don't say anything. It is not my place.

Chief Sasenticum agrees; Captain Smith and the other men will go on to Werowocomoco in the morning. I will stay in the Warraskoyack village and wait. If Captain Smith is killed, I will return to James Town to bring the news.

The next morning I watch the *Discovery* sail away with Captain Smith at her helm. I wonder if it will be the last time I see him. I push down sadness. I have already lost Reverend Hunt. I don't want to lose Captain Smith as well. I tell myself that he is wily and smart, and will not easily fall into Chief Powhatan's trap.

The Warraskoyack village is a busy place, and I want

to do my share of the work. But when I try to help two girls with their pounding of corn into meal, Kainta, Chief Sasenticum's son, pulls me away. "That work is for the women to do," he says. "I will show you men's work."

He takes me into the forest. There is a thin layer of snow on the dead leaves, and my feet crunch loudly on them. He stops and looks at me, frowning. "You are very loud," he says. He inspects my shoes. "My mother will make you moccasins."

He looks around, finds a sapling that seems to be just right for what he is searching for, and cuts it down with his hatchet. "I will teach you how to make a bow and arrows," he says.

Working with wood and stone is a good way to keep my mind off what might be happening to Captain Smith. Kainta teaches me how to peel the bark off the sapling, cut notches for the bowstring, and string it with strong gut. We make several arrow shafts from straight, thin wood. He shows me how to make an arrowhead, chipping a piece of rock until it is the right shape. It is a slow process, and I ruin several pieces of rock before I get it right, but finally I am able to make my first arrowhead. Then I tie it to a shaft and balance the shaft with feathers so that it will shoot straight.

When we grow hungry, we go to the communal cook fire. There we find a large clay pot filled with hominy and venison stew, fish on the grill and bread baking in the hot ashes on the ground. "Eat," says Kainta. He tears off a piece of bread and uses an oyster shell to scoop stew right out of the pot. I do the same. It is delicious. This is what I have seen people do all day, just come up to the pot and take what they want to eat. I realize that they have no mealtimes, no rationing of food, and I think that these Powhatan people must be the wealthiest people on the earth.

A young woman comes to put a new loaf of bread in the ashes and to stir the pot of stew. She wears a kind of apron made of deerskin that hangs down to her knees. Her arms, face, and legs have colorful tattoos of patterns, flowers, fruits, and snakes. Her black hair is plaited into one long braid hanging down to her hips. She smiles shyly at me. How strange I must look to her in my English clothes.

No messenger comes that day or the next. I don't know if this is good news or bad. I have no choice but to wait. At sunrise I go with Kainta down to the river where he bathes in the frigid water. I stay, shivering, on the shore. Kainta sprinkles a bit of tobacco on the river, closes his eyes, and lifts his hands, and I know he is praying. This is what Namontack did each morning when he lived with us in James Town.

The days go by, and I learn more about men's work, which is mostly about hunting and fishing. I am also careful to learn which chores are women's work so that I will not embarrass myself again by trying to do any of it. Planting, weeding, harvesting, making clay pots, cooking, making clothes—it is all for the girls and women to do.

Kainta teaches me how to make a knife by chipping a piece of rock until it is sharp, then tying it with gut onto a short stick. He gives me a buckskin pouch and shows me how to hang it from my waist with a leather strap. My knife fits nicely inside.

I continue to make my arrows, chipping the arrowheads and tying the feathers, until I have enough to go hunting. Kainta shows me how to weave a case so that I can carry my arrows on my back. He has me practice with my bow and arrows and a target until I can shoot straight.

It snows. Kainta says this will make hunting even easier because we will see the animals' tracks in the snow. I have my new moccasins, and I walk carefully, heel to toe, the way he has shown me, trying to be as silent as he is. I am concentrating so hard that at first I do not notice someone else who has been walking quietly in the forest. Then suddenly I look up and see him.

"Namontack!" I cry out. I am very glad to see him. Then, when I realize why he has come, I am filled with fear. He is the messenger from Werowocomoco.

I stand, gripping my bow, waiting for the bad news.

Namontack smiles. "Do not look so worried, Samuel. Your master sends good wishes."

I groan with relief. Then I am confused. "Why have you come and not Captain Smith?" I ask him in English.

He answers me in Algonquian. I am in his world now. "Captain Smith says you will stay with the Warraskoyacks through the winter. You will learn more of the language and eat well."

Kainta joins us. He and Namontack exchange the greeting of countrymen; with one fist, each taps first his own chest, then forehead, and then taps the other boy's chest and forehead.

"Come," says Kainta, "you must be hungry after your journey. We will hunt later."

We sit with Namontack at the communal cook fire as he eats. I form my question in Algonquian. "Chief Powhatan make trap?" I ask him. Now that I have heard the good news, I am ready to hear the whole story.

"Yes," Namontack says. "But your *werowance* is quick as a rabbit. The trap did not catch him." He grins. He likes Captain Smith as much as I do.

In between mouthfuls, Namontack tells us what happened. Captain Smith and his men arrived in Werowocomoco and were treated kindly. They traded for lots of corn, but by the time their boats were loaded up, the tide was out and the boats couldn't move. They had to spend the night in Werowocomoco, staying in one of the houses.

Just after dark Captain Smith heard a sound at the

door. It was Pocahontas. Her eyes were wide with terror. "You must go," she said. "In a little while my father's men will bring you food. As soon as you put your weapons down and begin to eat, they will slit your throats with your own swords! And if they don't succeed, there will be a bigger attack later." She begged them to leave right away. She was crying. She knew that if she was caught warning Captain Smith her father would have her put to death.

She may have been play-acting the first time, I think, *but this time she really did risk her life to save Captain Smith.*

The tide was still too low for them to leave. Within an hour, ten strong warriors came with platters of food, just like Pocahontas had said they would. The warriors said the slow matches on the English men's guns were smoking up the room, making them sick, and they should put them out. But Captain Smith just said, "Oh, we don't mind the smoke." Then he made the warriors taste all of the food to make sure it wasn't poisoned. Captain Smith and his men ate their supper with their guns smoldering and ready.

"And later, big attack?" I ask.

Namontack tells us how the Englishmen kept up a guard half the night, standing with their muskets ready. There never was an attack. At midnight the tide had risen enough to move the boats, and they left.

So Captain Smith and his men are safe. And they have

taken corn back to James Town. "Thank you—good news," I say to Namontack.

It has begun to snow again, and Namontack is invited to stay the night. He sleeps in the family house with Kainta and me.

The next day the three of us go hunting. We walk quietly through the white forest, stalking rabbits. We see one—even I have been quiet enough not to startle it. Kainta and Namontack both look at me. They want me to shoot, to have a chance to make my first kill. Silently I pull out an arrow and string it on my bow. I make my breath even and slow so that it will not affect my shot. I watch the rabbit as it hops along the undergrowth, looking for food. I pull back the bowstring and aim. Then I let the arrow fly. There is a whoosh and a thud—the arrow hits its mark. The hare lies still. Blood seeps out where my arrow has entered its side, staining the snow bright red.

Kainta claps me on the back. "You have learned well," he says.

I am still amazed at what I have done.

"Go, take your prize, and give thanks to the god Okeus for your meat," says Namontack.

I tie the rabbit's hind feet to a piece of gut and hang it around my waist. We hunt some more, and the other two boys also get rabbits. The winter day is short. When the sun sinks down, casting long shadows over glittering snow, it is time to return to the village.

I use my knife to cut open the rabbit's abdomen and clean out its entrails, and to peel the rabbit's skin away from the meat. My rabbit, which I have killed myself with a weapon I made myself, becomes part of the communal stew that evening. It makes me feel proud and strong.

Namontack goes home to Werowocomoco, and I stay at the Warraskoyack village, as Captain Smith has prescribed. Kainta and I do more hunting. He shakes his head when he sees me trying to keep my hair, which is getting quite long, out of my way. He asks his mother to cut my hair for me. She takes two mussel shells and grates away the hair on the right side of my head down to the scalp. It pinches and pulls, but I keep still. On the left side she leaves it long, and she cuts a ridge of short hair down the middle of my head so that my hair looks very much like the other men and boys.

"There," says Kainta. "Now it will not get caught in your bowstring."

When the winds of February blow cold, I wear a mantle of deerskin. During the March thaw I kill my first wild turkey. Kainta ties two of its feathers into the long side of my hair.

In late April when the mosquitoes, flies, and gnats come out, Kainta shows me how a layer of bear grease mixed with a powder of red puccoon root keeps the bugs away. It also makes my skin red. I no longer look very much like an English boy.

One day, we boys are playing a game that is much like English football. We have a goal at each end of a field, and we kick a ball made of skins, trying to score by kicking the ball into the other team's goal.

I have finally gotten tired of sweating in my slops and long-sleeved shirt during these games, and have let Kainta's sister make me a buckskin breechcloth to wear. The red puccoon dye protects my back, chest, arms, and legs from insects and the burning of the sun, and my moccasins protect my feet for running. The right side of my hair has been newly shaved by Kainta's mother, and the left side of my hair is quite long, almost to my shoulder. I've added a few shells to the feathers as ornaments.

As we play I hear a call of "*Wingapo!*" spoken with an English accent. I stop running. I have almost forgotten what English speech sounds like.

What I see takes my breath away. It is Richard, Nathaniel, Henry, Abram, and several others. They look thin and wan. They are walking toward us. Richard calls out, speaking Algonquian as if he has memorized just what to say. "Captain Smith send. Need eat. Find English boy, Samuel."

I sputter. "Richard," I call to him. "It's *me*."

Richard's eyes go wide and his mouth drops open.

"By God, he's turned into a savage!" Henry says.

I ignore Henry and go to greet Richard and the others. The Indian boys gather around us. "Are you here to bring me back?" I ask, still not understanding why they have come.

Richard shakes his head. "We're here to stay for a while to . . . eat. Rats got into the grain. There were so many of them they looked like maggots squirming in the barrels. We have almost nothing left. So President Smith has sent us different places: some he sent up the river to live on oysters, some down the river to Point Comfort to live on fish, and some to friendly tribes. We got sent here. We have copper to pay our way."

I translate as best I can for Kainta. He nods and says he will go tell his father that they are here.

"So"—Richard eyes me curiously—"did that stuff just get stuck in your hair, or did you put it there on purpose?"

I sock him playfully in the arm, and we both laugh. I think of how I want to teach him what I have learned—how to make snares to catch beavers, otters, and squirrels; how to build a fire in a canoe at night so the fish will be mesmerized and come close so we can spear them; how to find mushrooms and roots and berries that are good to eat. I know that with the knowledge I've gained from living with the Warraskoyacks, we don't ever have to be hungry again.

Twenty-Three

"What will it avail you to take that by force you may quickly have by love? Or to destroy them that provide you food? What can you get by war when we can hide our provisions and fly to the woods? Whereby you must famish by wronging us, your friends."

—Chief Powhatan, quoted in William Symonds, ed., *The Proceedings*

IF TROUBLE CAN multiply like rats in grain, then that is what our troubles do in 1609. By mid-summer, Captain Smith sends word to the Warraskoyack village that we are to return to James Town. A ship has arrived, so there is food. There is also much work to be done: We need to build houses for the new colonists. When I get to James Town, I am stunned by what I see. The Virginia Company has sent not only men but families with women and *children.*

Richard and I watch as two women meet in front of a cabin to talk for a moment. One holds a baby on her hip, and the other has a little boy of four or five clinging to her skirts.

I shake my head. "How could they do this?" I wonder out loud to Richard.

"It must be because no one is allowed to say anything bad about James Town in their letters back home," says Richard.

I nod. "The Virginia Company lies to them—about how it is paradise here, and how they will find mountains of gold. And they believe the lies."

The little boy sees us and grins around the thumb he has stuck in his mouth. I wonder if he will live through the winter.

It is strange for me to be living with Englishmen again instead of Warraskoyacks. Not even Namontack is with us anymore. It is hard to get used to eating only at mealtimes and having my food rationed again. I cut the long side of my hair and go back to wearing English clothes. I keep my bow, arrows, and moccasins in a corner of my cabin, but I still wear the buckskin carrying pouch with my knife inside hanging at my waist. Some nights I dream that I am back in the Warraskoyack village or hunting with Kainta and Namontack in a quiet, snow-filled forest.

It is good to see Ann and John Laydon again. When I first see Ann my jaw drops, and I think John must have been giving her all of his food rations along with her own, because she is very big around the middle. Richard sees my open mouth and elbows me so that I shut it before Ann sees.

"She's going to have a *baby*," he whispers.

I blush at my ignorance. I'm glad Richard warned me before I said something to embarrass her.

The ships keep arriving. The rumor is that the Virginia Company is tired of sending a few colonists and having most of them die off, so they are sending a lot, and women, too, so that even if many die, the colony will still survive. By summer's end we have nearly five hundred colonists to feed and house. We also have horses, cows, goats, sheep, more hogs, more chickens, and more dogs and cats. There is hardly room to step without landing on someone's foot, a squawking chicken, or a pile of cow dung. We cannot get the houses built fast enough, and we are crammed together almost the way we were on the 'tween deck of the *Susan Constant*. Arguments flare up nearly every day. The ships have also brought us back Captain Archer and Captain Ratcliffe. They make no secret of the fact that they hate Captain Smith and want to be rid of him.

There is a new charter, they say, sent by the Virginia Company. The charter says instead of a president and a council, we will have one governor to rule us. That governor is, for now, Sir Thomas Gates. Then, next year, Sir Thomas West, Lord de la Warr, will arrive to become our Lord Governor and Captain General. Sir Thomas

Gates is on his way to James Town on the flagship, the *Sea Venture*. "Step down from your office as president," they order Captain Smith.

Captain Smith demands to see this new charter. Captain Ratcliffe folds his arms over his chest. "It is on the *Sea Venture* with Sir Thomas Gates," he says. "You will see it soon enough."

But the days go by, and the *Sea Venture* does not arrive. Captain Smith insists he is still our president.

Now I see what it means that power is like weights in a balance, and when someone gains power someone else loses power. This Sir Thomas Gates, our new governor, has gained power even though he is still somewhere out at sea. And so, Captain Smith has lost power. The new colonists do not respect him. When he tries to explain our delicate relationship with the Indians, how we trade and work to keep a fragile peace, they scoff at him. "Those savages will understand the power in a musket—that's all they need to know," they say.

The day I see smoke rising over the treetops, I know something has gone terribly wrong. Two of the new settlers come straggling into the fort, dragging wooden clubs, their faces smudged with soot.

"Did you see that savage's expression when I lit up his house?" one man asks the other. He makes a mock terrified face and takes a few running steps, as if he is escaping something.

"Ha! And look at this," the other man says. "I found it in a house with a bunch of bones—as if the dead men could take it all with them!" He pours out the contents of a sack. Necklaces of shiny beads, copper, and tiny, beautiful shells go scattering over the ground.

I stare in horror. They have robbed the Indians' temples? Taken the jewels from the bodies of their dead *werowances*? Set their houses on fire?

"How many do you think we killed?" one is asking the other, holding up his club and examining it.

My legs go weak. The club is stained with blood. I don't stay to hear the answer, but run to Captain Smith's cabin. My throat is tight with rage, but I choke out the words. "The new settlers," I say. "They're killing and burning . . ."

Captain Smith marches to where the two men are still gloating, telling of their escapades to anyone who will listen. Captain Smith's glowering eyes silence the men at once. He demands to hear it all, and the men sheepishly give a full account. A group of our colonists have burned the natives' houses, stolen from their gardens, robbed valuables from their temples, beat the people with clubs, and shot them with muskets. The natives have become furious and killed some of our colonists. And so the Englishmen feel they have the right to do more killing and burning and stealing.

I want to shout at them. How could they do this?

They don't care that the natives have saved us from starvation over and over again. They don't care that Chief Powhatan himself saved us from freezing and hunger when all our houses burned. They have no hearts, only pride and a feeling that they are superior. They say the natives are savages, but in truth, these ignorant Englishmen are the savages.

Captain Smith is as angry as I am. "Are you trying to start an all-out war with the natives?" he shouts. "With ten thousand of them and a few hundred of us? Are you *insane*?"

I can see it in his eyes; the fury and the rage. He wants to punch something, beat someone's face in, punish the men who have done this. Then I see him do the same thing he did so long ago on the ship the day Master Wingfield ordered him arrested. He narrows his eyes. *He must be focusing his anger,* I think. He is devising a plan to try to change all of this.

"I will go up the river and talk to the tribes these men have wronged," he says. "I will work to make peace again. If I do not, it could be the end of our settlement."

Captain Smith gathers a few men to sail upriver with him in the shallop. He chooses several men who have been here since the beginning. Then two of the new settlers, both gentlemen, tell him how much they want to help make peace with the Powhatans. They badger Captain Smith to take them along. Finally, he relents.

I think these two gentlemen just want to get away from our crowded fort and go exploring. Then, a new thought strikes me: What if they are not just bored young men who want an adventure? What if they are under the influence of Captain Ratcliffe, Captain Archer, and the others who hate Captain Smith? What if they plan to do him harm?

The morning they leave, I watch the shallop sail away. There are six of them in the boat, and I am glad to see that three of the men are Captain Smith's trusted friends. Still, the uneasy feeling does not leave me.

Twenty-Four

Sleeping in his boat . . . accidentally [some]one fired his powder bag, which tore the flesh from his body and thighs nine or ten inches square in a most pitiful manner. But to quench the tormenting fire frying him in his clothes, he leaped overboard into the deep river where ere they could recover him he was near drowned.

—William Symonds, ed., *The Proceedings*

THEY SAY IT WAS an accident, no one's fault. Captain Smith lay down in the boat to take a nap. He was still wearing his powder bag. While he slept, a spark must have lit the powder bag—a spark from someone's pipe or from the slow match on someone's musket. The powder caught fire and exploded. It seared the flesh right off his leg. In agony, Captain Smith leaped overboard to cool the burn. His leg was so badly injured and he was so weak that he nearly drowned before the men could pull him out.

When Captain Smith comes back to us, he is crazed with pain, moaning in a delirium. Three men carry him into the fort. The flesh on his thigh is burned black and red, the skin hanging ragged and oozing. He is our fallen leader. And he has fallen all the way down.

The doctor gives Captain Smith medicine to ease the terrible pain and it makes him sleep most of the day. When he is awake, I bring him food and water.

When the doctor changes his bandages I give Captain Smith the handle of a wooden spoon to bite on so that he can endure the pain. I am surprised he has not bitten through the wood yet. It is awful to see him in so much agony. I wash his bandages, rinsing out the blood and ooze, and hang them to dry.

One of the soldiers tells me that before he was injured, Captain Smith was able to make peace with Parahunt, the *werowance* of a village that has been ransacked by our colonists. "But," the soldier confides in me, "the peace cannot last. There has been too much killing on both sides and everyone is too angry."

One day I bring Captain Smith a drink of water. As I help him to sit up, he goes pale and beads of sweat break out on his face. I keep hold of the goblet in case he blacks out.

"They have cut off my hands and cut out my tongue," he says in a hoarse whisper.

I shake my head. I don't know if he is fully awake or in a delirium. I want to tell him he still has his hands and tongue. "But, sir—"

"Go get Richard," he says.

I run down to the river where Richard is repairing fishnets. "Richard!" I call out. "Come quickly."

He splashes through the water to meet me. I am panting, out of breath.

"What is it—is it Captain Smith?" he asks.

"Yes. I mean no, he has not died. He is saying strange things. He asked for you."

We both run up the riverbank to the fort. We enter the cabin quietly.

"Sir, we are both here—me and Richard," I say.

"Good," he says without opening his eyes. He takes a deep breath as if he is gathering his strength. "They have taken away my power here," he says. "I can no longer use my hands and my words to help the colony. There is nothing more I can do. I will return to England."

His words hit me like a punch in the stomach. *Return to England?*

"Richard," he says, and Richard stands up straighter. "You will accompany me to England. I saw how you cared for Reverend Hunt in his illness, and I know you will do the same for me. We will leave with the next departing ship.

"Samuel," he says. He opens his eyes and turns his head to look at me. "You are one of the few original settlers left alive. I chose you for a reason. I knew how hard it would be here in the New World, and that only the toughest and strongest would survive. Reverend Hunt told me you were a fighter, full of anger and energy. I knew you would make a good settler, and you have. You will be fine here without me. You have your skills—building, farming, hunting, and you have your Algonquian language. You will stay because the colony needs you. I release you from your servitude."

I am too stunned to speak. I feel as though I have been dropped from a great height and have landed on my feet, but I don't know where I am. "But I am your page," I say softly. Who will I be without my master?

Captain Smith shakes his head and continues. "To make sure no gentleman decides to grab you up as his servant, I have apprenticed you to John Laydon. You will become a carpenter in your own right."

I am filled with both sadness and wonder. Reverend Hunt was right. I will not always be a servant. But Captain Smith and Richard both leaving me at the same time? It seems as if I have finally learned to be a friend, to open my heart and care. And now they will both be gone when the ships sail.

I take a deep, shuddery breath. "Yes, sir," I say. It is the only thing I can think of to say.

IN THE WEEKS before the ships are ready to leave, it is time to bring in the harvest, gather oysters, and bring in hauls of fish and meat and smoke it all so that it will last the winter. But without Captain Smith to lead us, the men shirk their work. And the gentlemen seem to have but one purpose in life: to make sure Captain Smith goes back to England as a man accused of many wrongs, rather than as a hero who saved our colony from extinction. They spend their time gathered in meetings, making lists of accusations against him. They do not even realize that Captain Smith's last act, making peace with Parahunt, has saved their skins—for now.

I feel as though there is a noose closing in around James Town, ready to strangle all of us here. Chief Powhatan is angry about the coronation fiasco. The new settlers have attacked Indian villages and made enemies where we used to have friends. We have too many settlers to feed, and yet hardly anyone is working to store food for the winter. And we are about to lose Captain Smith. I can see why Captain Smith wants to take Richard with him. Truly, only the strongest and toughest will survive what is coming. I wonder if I have what it takes.

There is one bright spot in all of this: Ann Laydon will soon have her baby. She is very happy to have other women here now, including a midwife, and children to hold and admire as she waits for her own to arrive. It will be the first child born in our colony. Ann says if it is a girl they will name her Virginia.

I have learned something important from Reverend

Hunt: When I lose someone, I should not close my heart to everyone, but should find someone else to fill the empty place. Captain Smith and Richard will soon leave, but I will still have my friends living nearby: Namontack, Kainta, and Pocahontas. And here in James Town, Ann and John Laydon are becoming like my new family. When their baby arrives, he or she will be like my little brother or sister.

"GET THE MIDWIFE! Now—quickly!"

A large woman, barely done tying her apron strings, goes running to the cabin John and Ann Laydon share with two other families. The men and children are ushered out, and we begin the long wait.

John Laydon paces, his face a mask of worry.

"She'll be all right," I tell him. But I know that birthing kills so many women—and babies—that John has reason to worry.

The hours tick by. I go off to chop some wood, then come back and wait with John. We hear screams from the cabin—Ann crying out in the pain of childbirth.

Finally, we hear the lusty wail of a newborn baby. John runs to the door of his cabin and pounds on it. "Let me in!" he demands.

"You wait," the midwife calls back to him. "And then you can see your baby girl."

John laughs and cries at the same time. "It's a girl!"

he exclaims. "The baby is alive and it's a girl!" Then his face darkens and he pounds on the door again. "And what of my wife?" he shouts. "Is she well?"

"Yes, yes. She was brave and she is well," the midwife announces.

John groans with relief. "They're both alive," he says, almost incredulous. "My wife and my baby girl."

A few weeks later, I am one of the first people Ann allows to hold baby Virginia. She is so tiny, so delicate. Her eyes move, looking at the ceiling above me, and she smiles sweetly, as if she is seeing angels. Ann says she's just making faces because she has gas. I offer Virginia my finger. She grasps it and holds tight. As I look at her, I feel sad. I feel the coming doom. How will she survive the hard times that will soon be upon us? Virginia blows bubbles and grasps my finger even tighter. "You must hold on this tightly to *life*," I whisper to her.

Twenty-Five

What shall I say? But thus we lost him, that in all his proceedings, made justice his first guide, and experience his second; ever hating baseness, sloth, pride, and indignitie, more then any dangers; that never allowed more for himselfe, then his souldiers with him; that upon no danger would send them where he would not lead them himselfe; that would never see us want what either he had, or could by any meanes get us . . . whose adventures were our lives, and whose losse our deathes.

–William Symonds, ed., *The Proceedings*

THE DAY THE SHIPS are to leave, I go to Captain Smith's cabin to help him gather his belongings. He is able to take a few painful steps with a cane now, but it is still hard for him to get around. Everyone says he is returning to England to get better medicine than we have here, but I know he would stay if they had not robbed him of his authority and his power to help our colony.

Captain Smith holds two strings of beads in his hand. They are a new kind—blue, with intricate designs made by layers in the glass. They are worth a fortune in trading because the Indians prize them so much. He looks at the beads sadly.

"I will not need these for now," he says. He holds them out for me to take. "Use them to trade this winter when the hunger sets in."

I am stunned. I have never before touched these New World diamonds. As a servant I did not feel I had the right to. Now I am no longer a servant. Slowly, I take the beads from him. They feel cold and smooth in my hand. I tuck them into the buckskin carrying pouch hanging at my waist.

Captain Smith looks at me hard. "Samuel, it will not be easy here. Things will happen that will make you angry. But do not let your anger get the best of you. *Channel* it—let it give you strength for what you can do to change things, to make things better. Do you understand?"

I nod. I have watched him do this over and over, this shifting of anger into calm action. "I understand," I tell him.

He looks around the cabin as if he is wanting to remember it always. My throat is tight with tears, but I will not let them fall. I remember the first time I saw Captain Smith on the docks at Blackwall, how strong and brash he seemed. I remember how I hated the idea of serving him and learning from him. Then I think of how much I *have* learned from him, how much I have changed because of him.

"I—" I search for the right words to say what I feel, but I can't find them. "I am sorry to see you go, sir," I say finally.

Captain Smith stands a little straighter. "I'll be back," he assures me. "I am not done with James Town yet."

Then he does something that surprises me almost as much as the beads. He reaches out his hand to shake mine—as if I am his equal. As if I am a man.

His hand is leathery and calloused from the hard work he has done here. So is mine, I suppose. We shake hands heartily. "Have a good voyage, sir," I say.

We begin the slow, painful walk to the ships, him with his cane and me carrying a sack of his belongings.

"I want to find you alive and well when I return, Samuel," he says good-naturedly. "No starving, no dying from the summer sickness, no getting shot full of arrows."

I grin. "Yes, sir," I say. His orders suit me just fine.

John Laydon joins us and gives Captain Smith a strong shoulder to lean on as he struggles to walk. "You have been a just leader, Captain," he says. "What will we do without you?"

"You experienced settlers know a thing or two about survival," Captain Smith says. "Maybe these newcomers will learn from you."

Others join us until we are a small knot of men walking slowly out the fort gates and down to the river. The men each have something to say: "You were the best president we ever had, sir." "You did more work than any of those gentlemen." "Who will trade with the natives with you gone, sir?" "Have a safe journey, Captain Smith."

The longboats are already making their trips back and forth to the mother ships. Richard is there waiting for his turn. He was still asleep when I left the cabin this morning, so this is the first I've had a chance to talk to him.

"Samuel," he calls to me as I approach. "Are you sure you don't want to come? Think of all you're missing—the seasickness, the rats, the storms, week after week in the nice dark 'tween deck."

I take a deep breath as if I am savoring my memory of the journey. "Ah, the stench, and the way the slop buckets sloshed all over the place in rough seas . . ." I touch my hand to my heart. "I *will* miss it."

Richard laughs. "Maybe you *should* come back with us," he says. "You can be an actor in one of Master Shakespeare's new plays."

There are plenty of good things I can think of about England: fields of heather blooming in the countryside; London's busy, exciting streets; the chance to visit my mum's grave. But I will stay here in James Town. I touch the beads through the soft buckskin of my carrying pouch.

"I suppose you'll miss me terribly, too," I say to Richard, continuing the foolery. "Who will you have fistfights with if I'm not there?"

He crosses his arms over his chest and we just look at each other. The truth is, I *will* miss him terribly.

"Richard, get yourself in that longboat or you're staying here," Henry shouts. He is helping with the launch and he has no patience.

There is no time for long good-byes. I ball up my fist and tap my chest, then my forehead, then Richard's chest and his forehead. "Good-bye, friend," I say.

Captain Smith and Richard ride the longboat to the ship. It is not easy for Captain Smith to climb the rope ladder to the deck, but Richard and some of the sailors help him, and he makes it. They turn for one last look at the Virginia shoreline and our fort and the group of us waving to them. Then they are ushered below to the 'tween deck for the long journey home.

SOON AFTER CAPTAIN Smith leaves, it is clear that we don't have nearly enough food to get us through the winter. When Chief Powhatan sends word that he will trade for corn, Captain Ratcliffe goes strutting around the fort, full of his own importance.

"I will take fifty men," he announces. "We have piles of copper and beads and we'll bring back plenty of corn to feed everyone. Captain Smith was not the only man skilled in trading. You will see how quickly we forget he was ever here."

The new colonists are happy. They trust Captain Ratcliffe, and they feel confident we'll be eating well all winter. But I still see that noose, ready to strangle our colony.

Then something happens that does give me hope—hope for me and John Laydon and his family. Master Percy says we will build a fort at Point Comfort, about thirty miles downriver from James Town, near where the river meets the Chesapeake Bay. From there we will be able to protect James Town from a Spanish invasion—we'll stop the Spanish ships before they even enter the river. Soldiers will work to pile up dirt and mount artillery. John Laydon and I are being sent to build cabins for the fort. We will call our fort Algernon.

I fear what will happen in James Town this winter, with its overcrowding and lack of food. And James Town is the heart of our colony. I believe that if the natives attack, it is James Town they will attack. But at Point Comfort we will have only about thirty men to feed. We'll have our own hogs, fish to catch, and oysters to dig. We will be just across the river from the Warraskoyack village where the people have become like my family, and very near the Kecoughtans who have been our friends because Captain Smith often stopped in to see them on his voyages. I have the blue beads and my Algonquian words. I will be very glad to spend the winter at Point Comfort instead of James Town.

I happily gather up my belongings for the move to Point Comfort. Then I go to the Laydons' cabin to offer to help them pack.

When I enter their cabin, John is packing up his carpentry tools. Ann is sitting quietly watching him while baby Virginia sleeps in her cradle.

"Are you already packed?" I ask Ann.

She looks down and shakes her head. John doesn't even glance at me.

I frown. "Why not?" I ask. "The barge will leave tomorrow morning."

"She isn't coming," John says quietly.

"What?!" I blurt out. "But you *have* to come!"

"No I do not," Ann informs me. "I finally have lots of other women here to talk to and help me with the baby. And I want to stay safe within the palisades, not out there in the open, unprotected from the Indians. John will come to visit me whenever he can. I will stay here in James Town."

I sputter, not believing what I am hearing. "It is *much* safer at Point Comfort," I tell her. "Our neighbors are the Kecoughtans, our friends, and the Warraskoyacks— I know everyone in the village by name. I can trade if we run short of food. . . ."

Ann shakes her head. "I have made up my mind," she says.

"You won't be safe within the palisade," I insist. "The

new settlers have made war with the Powhatans. John, tell her what it was like when we first got here, how we couldn't even step outside the palisade to hunt without being shot at, and men starved."

John stops working for a moment. "I told her," he says. "She is stubborn and knows what she wants."

"Then *order her* to leave James Town!" I nearly shout it.

John looks up at me, one eyebrow raised. I realize that I have said a stupid thing. It is not in his nature to order his wife to do something against her will. "She wants to stay with the other women," he says. "I won't take that away from her."

Ann crosses her arms over her chest and gives me a self-satisfied look. "Besides," she says, "our leaders are not at war with the Powhatans. Chief Powhatan just invited Captain Ratcliffe to come to Werowocomoco to trade. They will have a feast and entertain them with dances, just like you told me about. And they'll come back with lots of corn. We will have all we need to eat in James Town this winter. We won't even have to go out of the palisade."

I want to grab her and shake her, shout into her face, *There is no safety in James Town!* I am seething with anger—why can't they *see*? Why won't they listen to me?! I want to punch something. I ball up my fist, ready to slug the wall. Then an image flashes in my mind, of Captain Smith ready to lose control of his anger, then of him taking a deep breath, focusing, calming, devising a plan. I hear Captain Smith's voice in my head: *Samuel . . . do not let your anger get the best of you. Channel it—let it give you strength to change things . . .*

I take a breath, try to calm the fury inside me. I walk over to the cradle where baby Virginia is sleeping. She is wrapped in a blanket, her eyes fluttering in sleep, her little mouth making sucking motions. She is so new, so innocent. I look at Ann. She is young and innocent, too—only fifteen. And she is naïve—she trusts Captain Ratcliffe to keep her safe and fed. Suddenly it is Reverend Hunt's voice I hear in my head: *You must learn to make decisions out of love, not out of fear . . .*

I take another deep breath. My anger is focused. I have made a decision. I have a plan. I believe Reverend Hunt would approve—I have made this decision out of love.

I am about to steal a baby.

Twenty-Six

Good men did ne'er their country's ruin bring.
But when evil men shall injuries begin,
Not caring to corrupt and violate
The judgment seats for their own lucre's sake,
Then look, that country cannot long have peace,
Though for the present it have rest and ease.

—William Symonds, ed., *The Proceedings*

THE NEXT MORNING I am ready. My canoe, nestled in the rushes, has a bed of blankets, a jar of sweetened water, a clean rag, and a spoon for the baby, and a piece of bread saved from last night's supper for me.

I go to Ann and John's cabin. Ann is busy wrapping up dried beef and bread for John, and John is trying to comfort a fussy Virginia.

"Let me take her for a walk in the fresh air," I say. "Then you two can have some time together before the barge leaves."

John gladly hands Virginia to me. Ann ties Virginia's tiny bonnet on her and tells me to make sure I support her head. I promise that I will.

The fort is swarming with people. I walk by the crowds, out the gates, and just keep on going. I know there will be people outside the fort as well, so that my message will get back to Ann.

At the canoe, I am in luck. Two little girls are washing clothes in the river.

"Ooh, can we see Mrs. Laydon's baby?" one asks.

I tilt Virginia down so they can admire her, being careful to support her head.

"I am going to Point Comfort," I tell the girls as I climb into the canoe. "Mrs. Laydon will meet me there."

I imagine the ruckus when Ann discovers Virginia missing, and that these two girls will be in the middle of it, crying out in their high voices that they saw me and I said I was going to Point Comfort. I will have a head start by then, but I am sure that Ann will be on her way, following me. That is what I am counting on, that she will be on that barge with her husband. It will take hours to get to Point Comfort, but in my canoe I will be quicker than the barge, even with breaks to feed the child.

Virginia settles nicely on her bed of blankets and falls asleep as the canoe rocks in the water. I paddle out into the middle of the river, where a bit of current will speed me on my way. The trees on the shores have just begun to turn their autumn colors. The day is clear and warm, with a gentle wind. I have no fear of a storm blowing up to capsize us.

Three times I stop paddling when Virginia fusses to be fed. I spoon the sweetened water into her mouth. Then I dip the clean rag into the sweet water, give it to her to suck on, and she goes back to sleep. It is something I saw my mum do when she took care of a baby whose mother had died, until she could find a wet nurse.

It is late afternoon when we make it to the fort. I pull the canoe up on shore. Nathaniel is on watch along with another soldier, who is sound asleep. As I carry Virginia toward him, Nathaniel stares at me, openmouthed.

"Don't ask," I tell him. "I'll explain later. But please, can I put her in your tent?"

Nathaniel shakes his head. "I have to report you to Captain Davies, my commanding officer," he says.

I groan. "My meat ration for a month," I offer him.

His face lights up, and he leads me to his tent. I feed Virginia one more time and lay her down on a straw bed to sleep. She has wet through her blanket. I forgot all about diapers.

Then I go out to the waterfront to wait for the barge to arrive.

I KNEW SHE WOULD be angry. Furious, even. I am not prepared for Ann's rage when she arrives at Point Comfort.

"I'll kill you!" Ann shrieks. She runs at me, her hands raised. I try to grab her wrists, but she is too wild. Her fingernails rake my face. I feel stinging pain, see my blood drip.

"Let me explain!" I shout, but she is screaming too loudly to hear me.

"Thief! Murderer! Hang him!" she yells.

John disembarks as well. "Are you *mad*?" he shouts. He cuffs me hard. "You deserve to be hanged!"

I start to panic. I have stolen a child. *Will* they hang me?

"But she is safe," I say. "I did it to keep her safe. . . ."

Captain Davies takes me roughly by the arm. "Don't worry, Mrs. Laydon," he says. "He *will* be punished."

Ann is sobbing now. "Where is she?" she demands.

I see Nathaniel, looking terrified. He does not want to be part of this.

"I put her in Nathaniel's tent," I say quickly.

That is all they need to know. I am dragged off by Captain Davies as Ann runs to find her baby.

IT IS A MAKESHIFT brig but it does the job. Shackles on my wrists and ankles do not allow me to move much. There is no window, just cracks between the rough boards that let me know when the sun has set. I am left with a little water and the cold dirt floor to sleep on.

"For theft of the child Virginia . . ." What will my sentence be? Hanging? Whipping? I have seen whippings where at the end they are flogging a corpse. Captain Smith said he wanted me alive and well when he returned to James Town. I may not be able to follow through on my promise.

The worst of it is that I have failed. This has all been for nothing. Ann and Virginia will return to James Town tomorrow with the barge.

Since this may be my last night on earth I try to make my peace with God. *I am sorry,* I tell Him. Sorry that I failed with James and that now I have failed with Ann and Virginia. I hope that at least He understands that I meant no harm in stealing Virginia. I ask to please be taken up to heaven with my mum.

In the dark I huddle on the floor and wish for the peace of sleep.

"CAPTAIN DAVIES!"

The shout wakes me. It comes from the river. Morning light slants into my cell. I hear clumsy paddle strokes and realize someone must be approaching in a canoe. "Get Captain Davies—*now*!" The shout is closer.

I hear footsteps, voices, someone out of breath.

"It was a trap!" the man cries. The voices come nearer to my jail cell. I press my ear against the wall, hoping to hear. "Captain Ratcliffe and his men—only a few have escaped."

I listen as he describes the horror. The men were lured to Werowocomoco with promises of corn. Instead they were attacked, their throats slit. Captain Ratcliffe's end was even worse—he was tortured to death.

I crouch against the wall, straining to hear, but the voices fade as the men walk away. I shake my head in despair. More men dead, and no corn brought back to James Town.

A sound startles me—the scraping of the lock on the brig door. I get to my feet. It is time to face my sentence, and my punishment.

Twenty-Seven

Powhatan thus invited Captain Ratcliffe and thirty others to trade for corn, and having brought them within his ambush, murthered them.

—William White, *The Black Boys Ceremony*

POINT COMFORT, FEBRUARY 1610

SNOW FALLS, FINE as sugar, but inside our cabin it is toasty warm. I am about to get scolded, as usual.

"Samuel, what are you doing?" Ann stands with her hands on her hips.

"I'm hiding," I say simply. "Watch—she likes it when I pop my head out."

I drop the handkerchief, and Virginia erupts with giggles.

Ann shakes her head, but she is smiling.

I "hide" again. Virginia crawls to me, grabs the handkerchief, and pulls it away. She is so pleased with herself she laughs and claps her hands.

"Samuel, stop your playing and come help me," Ann says.

She needs more firewood. I do not hesitate, but jump up to do as she bids. I owe my life to her.

After she heard what happened to Captain Ratcliffe, Ann begged Captain Davies to retract my sentence. I don't know if I'd have survived the twenty lashes that were to be my punishment. Ann testified that I had done the right thing to convince her to be with her husband at Point Comfort. John, too, spoke up for me. He said I had meant well taking Virginia with me, and that he could not afford to lose his best apprentice. I owe my life to both of them.

I STEP OUTSIDE, leaving the warmth of our cabin. The air is crisp and sharp and smells of woodsmoke. Snow swirls, coating the tree branches and giving everything a hushed feel. I am wearing my moccasins, and so I walk lightly through the snow, quiet as Kainta taught me to be. I smile when I think of Kainta. When the river thaws, I will paddle across to visit him in the Warraskoyack village and trade for corn. In the meantime, the

Kecoughtans are very close by, and my blue beads have kept us well supplied with corn from them.

I go to the lean-to that protects our firewood from rain and snow, and stack the heavy pieces of wood in my arms. I feel strong. I *am* strong. I look around at the cabins that house our Fort Algernon soldiers—I helped to build every one of them.

Snow blows into my face and stings my cheeks, but I am warm. An image flashes in my mind of another wintry day, what seems like a lifetime ago, of me and Richard blowing on embers in a cold cabin, trying to coax up a fire. I feel a pang of missing him, and of missing Captain Smith, too, and Reverend Hunt.

Then my mind goes back further still, to a small fire in a friendly hearth and my mum bent over a pot, stirring. *I'm doing all right, Mum.* I send the words up to heaven to her. *I'm living with a family, with people I love. And we have food and fire. . . .*

The wind is blowing from the northwest, from James Town. I wonder if I can smell the smoke of their wood fires, more than thirty miles away, or if it is only our fort's fires I am smelling. The river has been frozen for many weeks now, and we have not heard from them. Are they as warm and well fed as we are, I wonder? A sudden chill makes me shiver. I feel it like a splash of cold water, that old sense of doom and dread, the fear that made me desperate enough to snatch baby Virginia away. I shake it off quickly. No sense worrying about James Town now—I have my duties here, and we are safe here.

Safe. The word settles on me like peace. Ann, John, and Virginia are here with me, and we are safe.

I load my arms with a few more pieces of wood, then turn and walk back through the snow to our cabin.

Afterword

Now all of us at James Town beginning to feel that sharp prick of hunger which no man truly describe but he which hath tasted the bitterness thereof. . . . All was fish that came to net to satisfy cruel hunger, as to eat boots, shoes, or any other leather some could come by. . . . And now famine beginning to look ghastly and pale in every face that nothing was spared to maintain life and to do those things which seem incredible, as to dig up dead corpse out of graves and to eat them.

—George Percy, *A True Relation of the Proceedings and Occurrents*

DURING THE WINTER of 1609–1610 the settlers at Point Comfort did not go hungry. They had enough extra fish and crabs that even their hogs were well fed.

As winter set in, ice formed on the river, and travel between James Town and Point Comfort became impossible. It was not until spring that those at Point Comfort found out about the horror that befell James Town that winter.

Chief Powhatan ordered his tribes to stop trading with the settlers at James Town. The natives also went to

Hog Island, which the settlers had stocked with hundreds of hogs, and slaughtered them all. Then they went back to killing any settler they found outside the fort. Settlers were afraid to hunt and fish, so they remained inside the palisades. When the stores ran out, and they'd eaten the last of their sheep and goats, they ate even the laying hens. As things got worse they ate their horses, dogs, and cats, and then any rat, mouse, or snake they could catch. When there was nothing left to kill, they even ate their starched collars, their leather shoes—anything that could be chewed and swallowed. Men, women, and children starved and died. Hunger caused desperation. Some of the colonists began to dig up the dead bodies and eat them.

One group of men escaped that terrible winter by using violence to secure a large quantity of food from one of the native tribes and then stealing one of the ships and sailing back to England. The remaining settlers were ravaged by disease, starvation, and warfare with the Indians. Out of the roughly five hundred settlers Captain Smith said were in James Town when he left, by spring only sixy settlers remained, all of them close to death. The winter of 1609–1610 became known as the Starving Time. Chief Powhatan had tried again to wipe out the "tribe" that came from the Chesapeake, and he had nearly succeeded.

In the spring of 1610, the man who was to be James Town's new governor in 1609, Sir Thomas Gates, finally arrived. He had been shipwrecked on Bermuda for nine months until new ships could be built from the remains of the *Sea Venture*. When Gates saw the desperate conditions in James Town he decided to abandon the settlement and take the remaining survivors back to England. But as they sailed down the river, heading home, they were met by a messenger carrying a letter. It said that Sir Thomas West, Lord de la Warr, the new Lord Governor and Captain General of James Town, was on his way up the river to James Town with three ships, over 150 new colonists, and food for a year. The message was clear: *Go back to James Town.*

Reluctantly, the settlers returned to try again. The next several years were difficult ones. James Town's new leaders took revenge on the natives, even the Kecoughtans and the Warraskoyacks, who had helped the settlers so much. They slaughtered native men, women, and even children from many tribes. Revenge bred revenge, and there were raids and killing on both sides.

In 1613, Pocahontas was kidnapped by the settlers and held hostage. In return for her freedom, they demanded that her father free the English prisoners he was holding, give back stolen English weapons and tools, and send a large quantity of corn. Chief Powhatan gave the settlers some of what they asked for, saying he would send the rest when his daughter was returned to him. The English said this was not enough. Chief Powhatan refused to give in to the hostage takers' demands, and Pocahontas remained a prisoner.

John Rolfe, a new colonist, began growing tobacco in James Town. Tobacco grew well in Virginia and sold well in England, and finally there was hope that the colony would make a profit for the Virginia Company of London. While she was held prisoner, Pocahontas met John Rolfe. The two were married in 1614, with Chief Powhatan's blessing. This began a period of time some historians call the Peace of Pocahontas. For a while, there was not as much bloodshed between the English and the natives, and the two groups shared the land together.

Pocahontas, her husband John Rolfe, and their son Thomas, were taken to England by Sir Thomas Dale to promote the James Town colony and help Dale get financial assistance. There she became ill and died in 1617. She was buried at St. George's Parish Church in Gravesend, England.

In 1619, the first Africans arrived in the Virginia colony on a privateering ship. It is not clear whether they were slaves or indentured servants, which means they would have to work for a number of years and then they would be free. But soon, especially with so much labor needed for the tobacco fields, Africans were brought to Virginia and sold as slaves for life.

Was Reverend Hunt's prediction right—did Samuel become something much greater than a servant? Yes. In

1619, the Virginia Company of London created the House of Burgesses in Virginia. By that time there were eleven settlements, and each settlement had its own leadership. Samuel Collier, by then a grown man, was recognized for his knowledge, skills, and ability to communicate with the natives in their own language. Captain Smith wrote that Samuel was appointed leader of a town.

Captain John Smith was never able to return to James Town. But his writings are one of our most valuable records of what went on in the colony.

Did the Powhatan prophecy ever reach its conclusion? In 1622, though Chief Powhatan had died, his empire was still strong, led by his brother, Opechancanough. There were still many more natives than Europeans living in Virginia, but more settlers arrived on ships from England every couple of months, and they were taking over more and more of the land the Indians used for hunting and planting. Chief Opechancanough decided to wipe out the English once and for all. He carefully planned his attack. On March 22, 1622, 347 colonists were killed—about one-third of the Virginia European population. The settlers began raiding the Indian villages, killing and burning, with the goal of exterminating the native people. War between the natives and the Europeans continued for years. Chief Opechancanough did mount one more large attack on the settlers, in 1644, but by then the European population had grown and the Indian population had been decimated. Chief Opechancanough was captured and killed, and the Powhatan empire crumbled. Just as the prophecy had predicted, the Powhatan empire was destroyed by a new tribe that arrived from the Chesapeake Bay.

During the first hundred years after the English arrived in 1607, over 90 percent of Virginia's native population was killed either in warfare and massacres or by the new diseases the Europeans brought with them. As Europeans took over more and more of their land, the natives were forced onto reservations, and then over time most of their reservation land was taken from them. There is, however, land in the Virginia countryside that, for thousands of years, has been home to the native peoples who still live there.

Author's Note

I GREW UP in Virginia, and so I studied the Jamestown story every time we covered state history. Then, in 2002, my historical novel *Storm Warriors* won the Virginia Jefferson Cup Award, and suddenly I was booked to speak at schools all over Virginia. I was wondering what to write about next, so as I visited these schools, I asked teachers and librarians for suggestions. "What would you most like to see a new novel about?" I asked. The answer came over and over: Jamestown.

I thought, *That old story? John Smith and Pocahontas AGAIN? Booooooring!*

That was before I started my research. When I looked into what really happened, looked beyond the dry textbooks I had studied as a child, I discovered a thrilling, exciting adventure story.

The challenge for me in writing historical fiction is always: how can I see, hear, feel, taste, smell, *know* what my main character experienced? Luckily for me, the entire Jamestown fort, the three ships, and a Powhatan Indian village have all been re-created at the Jamestown Settlement, complete with historical interpreters, gardens, muskets that really fire (without bullets, of course), corn that needs to be shucked, and all of the artifacts you can imagine. In addition to the Jamestown Settlement, the newly rediscovered original Jamestown fort is being excavated by archeologists. Every day they are uncovering pieces of pottery, building foundations, postholes from the original palisades, and even graves from the early Jamestown years. I spent day after day at these two sites, researching, asking questions, and generally absorbing the feel of it and trying to transport my imagination back in time nearly four hundred years.

At one point I decided to do a bit of reenacting myself, and so in May of 2005 I set up camp on the shores of the James River, not far from the original fort. The sights and sounds that greeted me at dusk, midnight, and sunrise gave me the feel of what Samuel Collier must have experienced that May of 1607 when the colonists first landed.

Of course, some of my research was book research, too. Several of the early Jamestown settlers wrote the story of their journey from England and of what happened here in the New World. Thank goodness, scholars came before me and took the "olde"-fashioned English spelling and modernized it so that it was much easier to read. Here is an example of what the original writing was like, taken from Sir Thomas Dale's June 10, 1613, letter from Henrico.

> If plenty of vyctulls wyll stope thes crused peoples mouths suerly this harvest beinge In, they wyll have in great aboundance, But If a greatter nunber be sent England must provyd bread corne, for them, untill they may reap of thes fruictes of ther owen labours.

Whew! I'm so glad I didn't have to read that kind of thing for hours!

Here is the modernized version, from Edward Wright Haile's book, *Jamestown Narratives: Eyewitness Accounts of the Virginia Colony.*

> If plenty of victuals will stop these crused [cursed] people's mouths, surely, this harvest being in, they will have in great abundance. But if a greater number be sent, England must provide breadcorn for them until they may reap of these fruits of their own labors.

It's still not the easiest thing in the world to understand, but that was where my job came in, using those original records, along with other sources, to create a story that could be understood and enjoyed by young readers in the twenty-first century.

Another note about spelling: English spelling in the early 1600s had not yet been standardized. People wrote phonetically, and when accents changed, spellings changed. (There were *no* spelling tests!) The same word was sometimes spelled in two different ways even in the same sentence. When it came to place names and people's names, variations became even greater. For example, I found eleven different spellings of the name Lord de la Warr: de la Warre, La-ware, De La Ware, Delaware, etc. And there are twenty-seven spellings of Warraskoy-ack! Even Jamestown changes its spelling (James Town, Jamestowne). I have tried to standardize the spellings of proper names within this book but you may see them spelled differently in other sources.

Working with original records is not always easy, especially when the same event is described by different people in different ways. For example, in Chapter Eight, I mention Fort Caroline, the French colony in Florida that was destroyed by the Spanish. There is a Spanish version and a French version of that incident. The Spanish said they killed 130 to 140 men and spared the lives of 50 to 60 women and children. The French said *everyone* was slaughtered, even the women and children. There is no way to know which version is correct, and I simply had to pick one when telling my story.

Another challenge in using original records is that sometimes they describe things that seem to be impossible, like the incident in Chapter Six where a swordfish and a thresher shark attack and kill a whale. This same incident was cited by not just one but two of the early settlers. William Strachey described the swordfish, "pricking" the whale in the belly "with his sharp and needle fin," and both Strachey and Percy described the thresher beating the whale with his fins, or "flails." And yet I have heard that fish don't act this way. Did it really happen as it was described? Or did these men misinterpret what they saw? Or . . . maybe the whole thing is just a fish story!

Speaking of fish stories, the modern-day Carib Indians say those stories about their ancestors being cannibals are nothing but lies. Some historians believe that the Europeans created the image of the Carib Indians as cannibals in order to justify the fact that they treated the natives so brutally.

One of the most controversial elements in the Jamestown narratives is the incident where Pocahontas laid her head over Captain Smith's head, protecting him from her father's warriors who stood over him, their clubs raised. Some historians believe that the incident never even happened. Others believe that Pocahontas really did save Captain Smith's life—that Chief Powhatan's warriors really were about to beat Captain Smith's brains out with those clubs. Still others believe in the "adoption ceremony" interpretation of the event. This is the one that made the most sense to me, and so I have used it in my story.

I do want to set the record straight about one thing: No matter what you have heard or seen in the movies, there is absolutely no evidence—not even a hint—that there was ever any romance between Captain John Smith and Pocahontas.

The Jamestown story is a story of culture clash, and this presented some challenges of terminology. For example, the English saw Pocahontas as a "princess" because she was the daughter of the Powhatan ruler (or, in the Englishmen's minds, the Powhatan "king"). But in Powhatan society, power does not pass through "royal" families from father to son or daughter the way it does in England. Instead, the line of succession went from Chief Powhatan to his brothers, then to his sisters, and then to his sisters' children. Pocahontas was not in line to inherit any power.

Another term that got my attention was this entry in early settler William Strachey's Algonquian/English word list: "*waugh*, their word of wonder." Compare to this entry in a modern-day Grolier's dictionary: "*wow*, used in expressing wonder." Jamestown historian Edward Wright Haile states that our word *wow* most likely comes from the Algonquian word *waugh*. (It's the same pronunciation—the British surname "Waugh" is pronounced "wow," so Strachey was just writing phonetically.) I know most dictionaries say that *wow* comes from old Scottish, but a whole collection of dictionaries will tell you that the term *powwow* comes from Algonquian and means, literally, "he dreams." It originally referred to a medicine man, or conjurer, whose domain was the world of wonder. Opinions will vary on this, but I tend to agree with Mr. Haile, that our word *wow* most likely comes from the Algonquian language.

This book, like my other historical novels, is a mix of what really did happen and what could have happened. All of the major events and most of the minor events are based on what happened on the journey from England and in Jamestown as described in the narratives written by the settlers themselves. All of the "characters," once the story leaves England, were real people.

Samuel Collier was a young boy who came to Virginia on one of the first three ships as Captain Smith's page. I did have to invent Samuel's backstory—his family life and origins. The records indicate that Samuel went with Captain Smith on two expeditions. The first was to Werowocomoco, in the fall of 1608, where the Indian maidens did their "warriors" dance. On the second expedition, en route to Werowocomoco, Samuel was left to live at the Warraskoyack village for a time. Samuel did stay in Virginia when Captain Smith left for England.

The four boys who came over on those first ships were Samuel Collier, Richard Mutton, James Brumfield (who really was just nine years old), and Nathaniel Peacock. One boy was killed in the first large-scale Indian attack in 1607, and it was neither Samuel nor Nathaniel, because their names appear on later lists. I had to choose either James or Richard to be the one who was killed in that attack, and I decided it would be James.

Though in some instances the dialogue is taken from the original records, for the most part I have invented dialogue, thoughts, personalities, and the like. And I have simplified a story that is far too complex to be contained in one book.

Descendants of the Powhatan empire still live in Virginia. To learn more about the Virginia Indians today, visit the Web site of the Virginia Council on Indians: www.indians.vipnet.org. There are eight state-recognized tribes: Chickahominy, Eastern Chickahominy, Mattaponi, Monacan Indian Nation, Nansemond, Pamunkey, Rappahannock, and Upper Mattaponi. Their culture is kept alive within their close-knit communities and is shared with the public through their tribal museums and celebrations at powwows that feature drumming, singing, dancing, and other traditional arts.

To read more in depth about Jamestown and the Virginia Indians of the past, I would recommend: *Love and Hate in Jamestown: John Smith, Pocahontas, and the Heart of a New Nation*, by David A. Price; *First People: The Early Indians of Virginia*, by Keith Egloff and Deborah Woodward; and *The Double Life of Pocahontas*, by Jean Fritz.

If you possibly can, go to Jamestown, Virginia, and see it for yourself! The following Web sites will help you plan either a virtual or real-time visit to Jamestown:

The Association for the Preservation of Virginia Antiquities: www.apva.org

Colonial National Historical Park: www.nps.gov/colo

Jamestown Settlement: www.historyisfun.org

FOR MORE INFORMATION about *Blood on the River: James Town 1607*, including a teacher's study guide, visit www.elisacarbone.com.

Acknowledgments

WITHOUT THE HELP of many people I would not have been able to gather the information and details required to make this story authentic. I have worked hard to make it as accurate as possible, and I claim full responsibility for any inaccuracies it still contains.

For guiding me through the research, answering my questions sometimes for hours, e-mailing me links and helpful information, brainstorming with me (also for hours), directing me to the resources I needed, reading the manuscript and giving valuable input, helping me find the answers to those little detail questions that seemed to be endless, and doing countless other things to help shape this book, I would like to express my deepest gratitude to Lee Pelham Cotton and Bill Warder of the Colonial

National Historical Park, Historic Jamestowne; Edward Ragan, Rappahannock tribal historian; William Schultz, Maritime Historical Interpreter; KLT and JJRT of the Jamestown Settlement; Eric Deetz and Tonia Deetz Rock, archeologists at the Jamestown archeological dig; David L. Perry, a Tuscarora Native American artist and activist of North Carolina; Nancy Egloff, historian with the Jamestown/Yorktown Foundation; Brenna Shanks, a librarian who was very helpful with British history; Joyce Krigsvold of the Pamunkey Indian Museum; fourth-grade teacher Jan M. Jones and her 2004–05 class at Mosby Woods Elementary School in Virginia; Joan Kindig, children's literature specialist; Claudia Putnam, writer and encouragement specialist; Lona Queen, who came up with the title; Dad and Mom, who were always available for brainstorming or reading yet another draft; my husband, Jim, for constant love and support; and Gail Karwoski, who wrote the *first* middle-grade novel about Samuel Collier (*Surviving Jamestown: The Adventures of Young Sam Collier*, Peachtree Publishers, 2001) and who was incredibly generous in directing me to the people, books, and places I needed to begin my research.

Many thanks also to the costumed historical interpreters at the Jamestown Settlement and the drummers and dancers at the Chickahominy, Rappahannock, and Upper Mattaponi powwows, who allowed me to film them for my school presentation slide show.

I want to thank my editor, Tracy Gates, for her encouragement, faith, and above all, expert guidance through the twists and turns as this story took shape. I also want to thank assistant editor Rachel Nugent for many valuable insights, editorial assistant Kendra Levin for excellent detail work, Kelley McIntyre for a wonderful job on the book design, and copyeditors Janet Pascal and Nicolas Medina for their meticulous attention to everything from grammar to historical facts.

Sources

Edward Wright Haile, ed. *Jamestown Narratives: Eyewitness Accounts of the Virginia Colony: The First Decade: 1607–1617.* Champlain, Virginia: RoundHouse, 1998.

David A. Price. *Love and Hate in Jamestown: John Smith, Pocahontas, and the Heart of a New Nation.* New York: Alfred A. Knopf, 2003.

CHAPTER ONE:
For primary source material about this prophecy, see William Strachey, *The History of Travel into Virginia Britannia: The First Book of the First Decade*, 1612, reprinted in *Jamestown Narratives*, pp. 662–63; and Uttamatomakkin (Tomocomo), "An Interview in London," reprinted in *Jamestown Narratives*, p. 881.

CHAPTER TWO:
George Percy, *Observations Gathered Out of a Discourse of the Plantation of the Southern Colony in Virginia by the English, 1606*, 1608?, reprinted in *Jamestown Narratives*, p. 85.

CHAPTER THREE:

Percy, *Observations Gathered Out of a Discourse*, reprinted in *Jamestown Narratives*, p. 85.

CHAPTER FOUR:

David W. Waters, "The Art of Navigation in England in Elizabethan and Early Stuart Times," 1958, extracted in *Love and Hate in Jamestown*, p. 21.

CHAPTER FIVE:

Percy, *Observations Gathered Out of a Discourse*, reprinted in *Jamestown Narratives*, p. 86.

CHAPTER SIX:

Percy, *Observations Gathered Out of a Discourse*, reprinted in *Jamestown Narratives*, p. 86. For another version of this account, see William Strachey, *A True Reportory of the Wrack and Redemption of Sir Thomas Gates, Knight, upon and from the Islands of the Bermudas*, reprinted in *Jamestown Narratives*, p. 398.

CHAPTER SEVEN:

John Smith, *The True Travels, Adventures and Observations of Captaine John Smith*, 1630, reprinted in *Jamestown Narratives*, p. 88n.

CHAPTER EIGHT:

Percy, *Observations Gathered Out of a Discourse*, reprinted in *Jamestown Narratives*, p. 90.

CHAPTER NINE:

William Symonds, ed., *The Proceedings of the English colony in Virginia since their first beginning from England in the year of our Lord 1606, till this present 1612, with all their accidents that befell them in their Journeys and Discoveries, taken faithfully as they were Written out of the Writings of Thomas Studley, Anas Todkill, Walter Russell, Nathaniell Powell, William Phettyplace, Richard Wyffin, Thomas Abbay, Thomas Hope, Richard Potts, and the Labors of Divers Other Diligent Observers that were Residents in Virginia*, 1612; as printed in John Smith, *The General History: The Third Book—The proceedings and accidents of the English colony in Virginia, extracted from the authors following by William Simons, Doctor of Divinity*, 1624; reprinted in *Jamestown Narratives*, p. 224.

(Note: The text of *The Proceedings* was written by several different settlers; William Symonds [Simons], who was not a settler, gathered and edited the writings for publication in 1612. Later, when Captain John Smith published *The General History: The Third Book*, he included much of the text of *The Proceedings*. Therefore, quotes from the text of *The Proceedings* are often attributed to Smith, since his name is on *The General History: The Third Book*. Unfortunately, this has done a lot to create an image of Captain Smith as self-aggrandizing, since some of these quotes praise his leadership, work ethic, courage, etc. It is difficult to attribute specific passages to specific authors among the authors of *The Proceedings*, but the important thing to note is that Captain Smith is not the author of *The General History: The Third Book*.)

CHAPTER TEN:
John Smith, *A True Relation of such Occurrences and Accidents of Note, As Hath Hap'ned in Virginia, since the First Planting of that Colony*, 1608, reprinted in *Jamestown Narratives*, p. 146.

CHAPTER ELEVEN:
Symonds, *The Proceedings*, as printed in *The General History:*

The Third Book, reprinted in *Jamestown Narratives*, p. 225.

CHAPTER TWELVE:
Edward Wright Haile, "Virginia's Indian Contributions to English," reprinted in *Jamestown Narratives*, pp. 79–82; John Smith, *A Map of Virginia with a Description of the Country, the Commodities, People, Government and Religion*, 1612, reprinted in *Jamestown Narratives*, pp. 79–82 and 208–9.

CHAPTER THIRTEEN:
Edward Maria Wingfield, *A Discourse of Virginia per Edward Maria Wingfield*, 1608?, reprinted in *Jamestown Narratives*, p. 192.

CHAPTER FOURTEEN:
Symonds, *The Proceedings*, as printed in *The General History: The Third Book*, reprinted in *Jamestown Narratives*, p. 231.

CHAPTER FIFTEEN:
Symonds, *The Proceedings*, as printed in *The General History: The Third Book*, reprinted in *Jamestown Narratives*, p. 240.

CHAPTER SIXTEEN:
Smith, *A True Relation*, reprinted in *Jamestown Narratives*, p. 164.

CHAPTER SEVENTEEN:
Christopher Newport, Letter to Salisbury, 29 July 1607, reprinted in *Jamestown Narratives*, p. 130.

CHAPTER EIGHTEEN:
John Smith, *The General History of Virginia, New England, and the Summer Isles: The Fourth Book*, 1624, reprinted in *Jamestown Narratives*, p. 864.

CHAPTER NINETEEN:
Symonds, *The Proceedings*, as printed in *The General History: The Third Book*, reprinted in *Jamestown Narratives*, p. 314.

CHAPTER TWENTY:
Symonds, *The Proceedings*, as printed in *The General History: The Third Book*, reprinted in *Jamestown Narratives*, p. 281.

CHAPTER TWENTY-ONE:
Symonds, *The Proceedings*, as printed in *The General History: The Third Book*, reprinted in *Jamestown Narratives*, p. 281.

CHAPTER TWENTY-TWO:
Symonds, *The Proceedings*, as printed in *The General History: The Third Book*, reprinted in *Jamestown Narratives*, p. 296.

CHAPTER TWENTY-THREE:
Symonds, *The Proceedings*, as printed in *The General History: The Third Book*, reprinted in *Jamestown Narratives*, p. 299.

CHAPTER TWENTY-FOUR:
Symonds, *The Proceedings*, as printed in *The General History: The Third Book*, reprinted in *Jamestown Narratives*, p. 332.

CHAPTER TWENTY-FIVE:
Symonds, *The Proceedings*, reprinted in *Love and Hate in Jamestown*, p. 122. Written about Captain Smith when he left the colony, by colonists Richard Pots, William Phettiplace, William Tankard, and G.P.

CHAPTER TWENTY-SIX:
Symonds, *The Proceedings*, as printed in *The General History: The*

Third Book, reprinted in *Jamestown Narratives*, p. 226.

CHAPTER TWENTY-SEVEN:
William White, "The Black Boys Ceremony," as printed in Samuel Purchas, *Purchas His Pilgrimage, or Relations of the World and Religions Observed in All Ages and Places, Etc.*, 1613, reprinted in *Jamestown Narratives*, p. 141.

AFTERWORD:
George Percy, *A True Relation of the Proceedings and Occurrents of Moment Which Have Hap'ned in Virginia from the Time Sir Thomas Gates was Shipwrack'd Upon the Bermudes, Anno 1609, Until My Departure Out of the Country, Which Was in Anno Domini 1612*, 1625?, reprinted in *Jamestown Narratives*, p. 505.

Many of these primary sources may be accessed on the Internet.

www.americanjourneys.org/texts.asp
Includes the complete texts of Smith's *A True Relation* and Percy's *Observations*.

www.virtualjamestown.org/fhaccounts_desc.html
Offers many primary texts, including writings of John Smith, George Percy, Edward Wingfield, and Lord de la Warr.

www.arches.uga.edu/~iyengar/Strachey.html
Includes excerpts from William Strachey's "A True Repor

www.winthropsociety.org/texts.php
Includes several excerpts from Smith's writings

cc
Tarot

CH
Sy

EDISON JR. HIGH LEARNING CTR.